ALSO BY HENRY BROMELL

The Slightest Distance

I KNOW YOUR HEART,
MARCO POLO

I KNOW
YOUR HEART,
MARCO POLO

stories by Henry Bromell

 Alfred A. Knopf, New York, 1979

THIS IS A BORZOI BOOK PUBLISHED BY ALFRED A. KNOPF, INC.

All of the stories in this book originally appeared in *The New Yorker*.

Grateful acknowledgment is made to the following for permission to reprint
previously published material:
Al Gallico Music Corp.: An excerpt from the song "House of the Rising Sun."
Copyright © 1964 by Keith Prowse Music Pub. Co. Ltd. Used by permission.
Big Sky Music: An excerpt from "Lay Lady Lay" by Bob Dylan. Copyright ©
1969 by Big Sky Music. Used by permission. All rights reserved. An excerpt
from "I Threw It All Away" by Bob Dylan. Copyright © 1969 by Big Sky
Music. Used by permission. All rights reserved.
Unichappell Music, Inc.: An excerpt from "Don't Be Cruel" by Otis Blackwell
and Elvis Presley. Copyright © 1956 by Elvis Presley Music, Inc. & Travis
Music Company, Inc. All rights controlled by Unichappell Music, Inc. & Travis
Music Company, Inc. International Copyright Secured. Used by permission.
All rights reserved.

Library of Congress Cataloging in Publication Data
Bromell, Henry. I know your heart, Marco Polo.
CONTENTS: Partial magic.—I know your heart, Marco Polo.—The world in
a room.—Travel stories.
I. Title.
PZ4.B86814Iak[PS3552.R634] 813'.5'4 78-3580
ISBN 0-394-50116-0

Manufactured in the United States of America

First Edition

For my brothers

CONTENTS

Partial Magic

WE called him Lightning Joe because when he was young and courting Mabelene Murdock lightning struck the willow they were standing under and left him a stillborn husband. Or so the story went. We used to watch him, Sunday mornings, dancing down King Street, a striped railroad cap on his head, calling, "Mabelene! Mabelene!" Larry would laugh, his younger brother Johnny laughed, sometimes I laughed, and, seeing me, my little brother Matthew must have laughed—we probably all laughed. There was also an old man who stood, those Sunday mornings, on the corner of King Street and Patrick Street, a black camera propped before him on a wooden tripod. For a dime, he'd take your photograph, his uneasy eyes disappearing under the black cloth as he snapped the shutter. He and Lightning Joe often shared a bag of peanuts while they watched the church cars glide silently along the street, Joe talking and talking, the old man listening, the gang—the Untouchables—still laughing as we ran back to the alley behind Prince Street, turned cardboard boxes into tanks, and fought wars that lasted years. Only Larry wouldn't play. He preferred to strum his cracked guitar and sing "Love Me Tender" and "Heartbreak Hotel." A silver medal dangled from his neck, a medal the Air Force had given his mother after his father was killed in Korea. Though he was my age he seemed to me older, more graceful and competent, a strong, slight soldier who ruled the alley and protected us from Pig, the neighborhood bully. He and I used to walk to school together,

over the brick sidewalks buckled by frost, past the railroad tracks, where fires burned in ashcans, and through the
maze of new apartment buildings, raw and defeated in the
green morning light. Recess found us on the same kickball
team, and we spent evenings roller skating, until darkness
descended, or playing in that alley. One summer night, for
trivial, tactical reasons I no longer remember, Johnny and I
started fighting. Because Larry was there, watching, I wanted
to win, I didn't dare lose, I fought fiercely until I
heard him shouting, "Come on, Johnny, beat him!" My
desire drained away. Johnny surged with need, the need to
win for his brother. He grew stronger, I grew weaker. At
the same time, as I felt this delicate exchange of strengths,
I wanted to please Larry by letting Johnny win. Bits of
broken glass and rock gouged my back as Johnny triumphantly pinned me down, his knees on my shoulders. "All
right, knock it off!" my father bellowed, striding into the
alley. "Scobie, inside." Larry looked small and helpless as
he retreated, respectfully, into the shadows beneath the old
willow. Matthew and I took our bath, ate dinner in the
kitchen, wearing pajamas, and climbed the stairs to our
room at the top of the house. Through the open window
we could hear other boys, including Larry, still playing kickball under the streetlights, the ringing bell of the ice cream
truck as it drove slowly down Prince Street. Matthew slept
soundly, a tattered stuffed animal clasped in his hands.
Older kids parked their cars by the curb and turned up their
radios. The songs rising through the night carried me to
the outskirts of Alexandria, where willows and swamps
pressed against the chain-link fences of barren backyards.
There, I imagined, the highway began, sweeping from the
city and stretching into darkness. I stared at the ceiling so
hard it vanished. Cats screeched in the alley. A train ran over

a penny. Peering down through metal and wires into the light beneath a chassis—this must have been a dream—I could see my father's hands, flecked with oil, slowly tightening a nut. He swore as his hand slipped and slammed against the axle. "Pass me that wrench, will you, Scobie? It's on the bench, I think. You're not very interested in cars, are you?"

"No, sir."

"Well, no matter. I understand you've started writing."

"Yes."

"Is it fun?"

"I guess."

"Best reason in the world to do anything. For the sense of satisfaction when you're done. Now, can you reach in here? See that little round thing? Hold that while I tighten up."

By the time we were thirteen Larry and I were both in boarding school, a cluster of green-shingled houses built on the side of a mountain in the nineteen twenties as an insane asylum for the rich. I used to feel like an Indian as I walked up the hill from football practice, breathing the light September air. A rattle of silverware floated from the kitchen window of Gibbs Hall. Every Sunday, dressed in suits, we all gathered around the flagpole, then followed Mr. Pritchard, a large, white-haired man, down the mountain to church. As we walked he pointed out, with his ivory cane, the flora and fauna. The steep winding road took us past the glass auditorium and a graveyard filled with worn gray headstones, under the railroad bridge, across the highway, and into town, a perfectly still and beautiful monument to a vision I'd already betrayed: purity, God's watching presence. After church Larry always held his breath as we passed back under the railroad bridge. It brought him good luck, he said. Afternoons, we tossed a football or climbed the mountain to a view of small white houses, square fields that looked like maps of fields, the slim church steeple, vague blue hills across the valley. What was it that set Larry apart? Why did even his clothes seem different? And why did no one resent him for being unique and knowing it? He'd grown taller, thicker through the shoulders. Somehow he managed not to spill food on his tie, which I always did. He spoke seldom and carefully. Younger students admired him, teachers respected him. "A born leader," Mr. Pritchard called him. What Mr. Pritchard didn't know, what no one knew, was that after lights Larry and I took turns pretending we were women, Larry lying quietly beneath me, holding my shoulders, then leaning above me, his face cautiously happy in the half-dark. He had a way of tilting his head to one side when he was puzzled or shy that reminded me of my grandmother. His skin smelled like warm milk. His lips, touching mine, were soft and damp. Leaves drifted past the window. Would I ever know a real woman? Larry left the bed, reached into a hole he'd cut in the wall behind his bureau, and returned with his bottle of Jack Daniels. The dark night slowly filled with wind. Larry tucked his knees to his chest. Neither of us spoke, we just drank until we couldn't stop giggling, then dressed and veered on tiptoe down the quiet corridor and out into the wind. We crossed the hill behind our dormitory, sat down, our heads tossed back, and stared at the stars. "I'm going to California," Larry said. "Join a rock-and-roll band." Standing, he raised his arms to the sky, looked at me, smiled, and started running toward the distant line of trees, drunkenly agile, merging with the darkness, vanishing. "I dreamed I was laughing with Dad," he told me one day, knotting his striped tie in the mirror. "I couldn't see his face. I kept trying, but all I could see was his shape, kind of blurred, by the window at home." The pipes rattled, the radiators clanked, the shouts of other boys echoed in the dormitory. I followed him out into the cold light, stopping when I heard the line slapping the flagpole, almost remembering something. We reached the class building just as the bell rang, hurried down the hallway through the smells of wet overcoats and hair tonic and chalk. "Good afternoon, gentlemen." Mr. Pritchard stared skeptically over the top of his glasses. "I'm glad you decided to join us." We sat down to laughter and opened our spiral notebooks. " 'That's my last Duchess painted on the wall,' " Mr. Pritchard intoned. " 'Looking as if she were alive.' " I wished Larry weren't there. His presence, so physical, reminded me of our sick and secret life. I was sweating. " 'She had a heart—how shall I say?—too soon made glad.' " A prefect suddenly appeared in the doorway. Mr. Pritchard ambled over, hands in his pockets, and listened as the prefect whispered in his ear. They looked like two bargaining merchants, or priests. I could see the trees outside shaking in the wind. The prefect left and Mr. Pritchard returned to the front of the classroom. He sat down on the edge of his desk, took off his glasses, peered out the window, cleaned his glasses with his tie, cleared his throat, stood, thrust his hands back into his pockets, and looked at us. He was crying. "President Kennedy is dead," he said. "He was assassinated this afternoon in Dallas."

Forgotten intentions meandered, then straightened into King Street, an orderly approach to the giant white tomb, the Masonic Temple planted on a hill. Along the way stretched People's Drug Store, Penney's, Cohen's Hardware, pawn shops and pool halls. Alexandria. Such an exotic and strangely appropriate name. Over the years urban renewal created a new town hall, colonial streetlamps, and a large brick square, dominated by a fountain, where drunks and juvenile delinquents passed away the long summer days. Lightning Joe disappeared. The old photographer disappeared. My family moved to Jordan, then Kuwait, my father attached to the embassy there. Our house was sold. But I still came back for vacations with Larry. It seemed to rain most of the time, a light tapping of drops on the windowpane. Staying alive, Larry's mother had somehow betrayed him, so he never spoke of her, only of his dead father, the few memories he had and the impression he'd imagined, a portrait I in turn corrupted of an only child, a high school athlete, a martyred pilot, a quiet, serious man with a secret he'd never had time to tell his son. When it rained, the streets turned bright gray. The old brick houses nodded in their rows. I walked through the city, peeking like a spy into all the windows. A small black boy, compact in his sneakers and bluejeans, balanced precariously along the wall outside Giant Food Store. Girls in green kneesocks and plaid skirts, enormous textbooks pressed to their breasts, strolled the streets after school— girls we'd known since childhood who now invited us to basement parties, their squinting, nearsighted eyes already looking for husbands. We rarely went. Instead we sat in Larry's room, listening to records or talking. We no longer touched. That was over. When it snowed the city grew soft. Footsteps were silent on the brick sidewalks. Hulking yellow trucks nosed along Prince Street, tire chains clanking

like tanks. Across the river, Washington glowed, a monu-
mental ghetto approaching through the storm. "Let's go to
Paris this summer," I said, watching the snow blur and
mist beyond the windshield of Larry's car.

He glanced at me as we circled Lincoln Memorial. "You
know anyone there?"

"Sure. The Taylors. You must have met Alice. Her family
lives there."

"So let's go," he said. "Let's save our money and go."

Shimmering black faces stared at us as we parked the car
and filed into the Coliseum. I'd been here as a child to see
the circus. Now, instead of laughter, there was screaming,
and the tension was as thick as heat. Policemen linked arms
and formed a passageway from one of the bathrooms to the
stage. The lights went down. Dressed in collarless gray
suits, the Beatles appeared, their hair not as long as I'd
expected, their faces nervous and shiny with sweat. The
screaming was so loud and persistent it became a noise in
my head, a noise that seemed to have nothing to do with
what I was watching. When the first chord of "I Want to
Hold Your Hand" screeched through the speakers, the
screaming climbed still higher, pitched to shatter, release
me from whatever force had dressed me in loafers and
chinos and button-down shirt. Hundreds of girls rushed the
stage, crushed against the police, gasping and weeping.
Everywhere I looked people were on their feet dancing. I
danced with the girl next to me. She was in a trance, her eyes
unfocused. The pulsing darkness sloped down to a single
circle of light above the stage. Screaming obscured all but
the beat, the motion, the throb, yet I heard, distinctly, a
scream behind the screaming, a scream rising in my own
throat and flying loose and joining thousands of identical

screams high above me and then pushing down with all the power of music and a kind of cruel joy. I was shouting, dancing, my hands in the air. Larry, however, remained slouched in his seat—silent, unexcited, frowning. After-ward, we stumbled out into the muffling snow and drove back to Alexandria.

"They're not as good as Elvis," Larry murmured.

"Oh, they're better," I said. "Much better."

Larry hunched above the wheel, smoking a cigarette, his eyes staring down the tunnels of light drilled through the falling snow by our headlights.

We flew to Europe in June, landing in London, buying bicycles, then taking the Channel ferry to Calais. It was dark when we arrived. We wheeled our bicycles along the narrow, cobbled streets until we found a cheap hotel, a damp stone house with shuttered windows and dark furniture. Our single bed sloped in the middle. I clung to the edge and remembered sleeping in my grandfather's bed—my mother's father—just after he died. A similar de-pression, the shape of his absent body, had kept me awake all night, listening to the taxi horns far down on Park Avenue. If I fell asleep and let myself roll back into that cavity, that hole, I'd disappear too, I'd never stop falling. When I awoke the next morning brilliant white light filled our room. Larry still slept. I jumped from bed, my back stiff, and hobbled to the window. There, real for the first time, were the pink tile roofs, the crooked chimneys, the cooing gray pigeons, the leafy treetops of France. "Let's go, Larry," I called, quickly dressing. "Come on." Salt sea air and the smell of fresh bread mingled at the window.

Larry followed me out onto the sidewalk, smoked a
Gauloise, coughing, while I sipped café au lait and watched
the citizens of Calais move along the street carrying string
bags of fruit and books. I expected Nazis to step into the
square and arrest me. By the sea, surrounded by sand dunes,
we discovered a windowless concrete building with hooks
in the ceiling and the riddled shapes of men, arms out-
stretched, cut in the walls by bullets. Lying in my sleeping
bag, I waited for American ghosts to storm Omaha Beach,
their pale eyes locked in a look of sudden recognition
as they collapsed to the sand. Larry's skin burned brown,
golden. His hair, bleached and uncombed, curled extrava-
gantly. We patiently bicycled up and down hills, stopping
in yellow meadows to eat our cheese and bread and drink
red wine. For the first time in my life I felt free. But Larry
wanted more. "I hate school," he said, lying with his hands
behind his head, clouds mirrored in his eyes. "I've got to
get out. I want to travel. See the world. Fall in love with a
Russian ballerina." Nearing Paris, pedaling hard, we were
mistaken for riders in the Tour de France. Crowds lined the
streets and clapped, offering us cold water and waving en-
couragement. We stopped in front of a café to let a herd
of sheep pass. Suddenly Larry jumped off his bicycle and
ran inside. "Larry, what's wrong?"

"Diarrhea," he moaned from the other side of the
varnished bathroom door. "I'm dying."

"You're not dying, for godsake."

"Scobie, seriously. I can't go any farther."

I asked one of the waiters if I could call Paris, and as I
waited for the line to ring I listened to my voice's echo:
You're not dying, for godsake. The tone, such irritation,
surprised me. "Hello? Mrs. Taylor?"

"No, this is Alice."

"Alice? This is Scobie Richardson."

"Scobie! Where are you?"

I named the village. "Larry's—my friend's sick. We're stuck. Help, I guess, is what I'm saying."

"Momma!" I heard her hand cover the telephone. Her voice returned. "All right. There's a large square in the center of the village. Wait there. We'll see you in about an hour. Scobie?"

"Yes?"

"I'm glad you're here."

The telephone clicked into buzzing silence. For a few seconds I stood staring at the receiver. What had she meant by that? Then I thanked the waiter and found Larry. He was better but weak. We walked our bicycles to the square. A flower stall bloomed on the corner. Café awnings and umbrellas shaded the sidewalk. An airplane wrote P E R N O D in the sky. Larry brooded. "I'm sorry," he said.

"Don't worry. It's not your fault."

He stared at his feet. "Do you like Alice?"

"I don't know. I haven't seen her in a while. She's silly, I think."

"Is she beautiful?"

"No," I said.

The Taylors lived in Neuilly in a long, cool apartment fronted by a small garden, a gravel walk, and a green metal fence. Alice moved through the shadowed rooms as if they were cobwebs, always waving something away, her dark eyes never quite meeting mine. Her mother spent most days reading in bed, her flat, almost prehensile hands turning page after page. I rarely saw her father. He was a tall man with a graying beard and a quick smile who, like my father, worked for the State Department. Timmy, Alice's younger brother, lived in a world of cameras, sailing boats, and mountain climbing, silent and shy until Alice invited a schoolmate to stay—Rebecca, a hazel-eyed prodigy whose father made flags. Timmy fell in love with her but she ignored him, casually breaking his heart. Larry and Alice didn't get along, either. He was always arguing with her, making fun of her enthusiasm, speaking of her contemptuously when he and I were alone. Accompanying Alice and Rebecca as they took their daily walk in the Bois de Boulogne to smoke cigarettes, I felt excluded by their friendship. They seemed to speak a secret language of significant pauses and sudden hilarity. Alice wore bluejeans, sandals, a gray sweatshirt. " 'So sister, go tell your brother, not to do what I have done,' " Rebecca sang. We wandered from one end of the Bois to the other, circling ponds, watching children launch their sailboats, the kites that hovered above the trees like red and blue birds. The degrees of greenness, the many-hued strokes, rose behind Alice and drew her in, her eyes glancing at me from flowers. A girl ran by, rolling a hoop with a stick, laughing. I hunched my shoulders, Heathcliff, Byron, Mick Jagger. Paris mornings were pink, soft and glistening after the rain. Afternoons seemed endless, hot, still, only the distant rumble of traffic disturbing the lucent quiet. At night, Algerians beat their small drums along the Seine. Sitting cross-legged on the living room couch, Larry tossed his book aside and stared at the Cambodian tapestry, the marble ashtrays, the Picasso lithograph. It was late. He and I were the only ones awake. Radio Luxembourg played the Zombies. "I'm leaving," he said, looking at me.

"What?"

"I'm leaving."

"You're crazy."

"I don't like Paris. I'm sick of culture. I'm sick of all this *age*. It's just like boarding school. I'm going to California."

"Sure you are."

"Wait and see."

"Larry, why?"

"I told you, this place gives me the creeps. And I don't get along with Alice. You know that." He leaned forward. "Come with me."

"I can't. We just got here."

"You like all this death?"

"It's not death, Larry. It's beauty."

"Same thing. Leave."

"I can't," I said again. "I want to stay."

"Okay. So stay."

He bent down and investigated his toes, a habit I hated. I'd welcome his leaving. Yet when the time came I almost changed my mind. He laughed and told Rebecca he'd buy one of her father's flags as soon as he got home. He shook hands with Alice and Timmy. All around us people hurried toward their flights. Garbled French voices announced arrivals and departures. "See you later," he said, touching my shoulder. "Take care." He joined the line of travelers pushing through the glass doors. He turned, once, and waved. Then he was gone. From the observation deck, I watched his airplane rise higher and higher until it was just a dark spot in the sky.

Sometimes, late at night, when I can't sleep, I lie here in the dark remembering those days after Larry left, the lamps of the small shops burning into evening, jewelers and merchants working late, their voices carrying into the streets thronged with strolling couples, tired businessmen, students on the prowl, bewildered tourists. I have a wife now, quietly dreaming beside me, and a child. I live in a house of my own. Larry is dead, a victim of the sixties, heroin in particular, and Alice writes me occasionally from Cincinnati, where she and her husband, a lawyer, are raising their two girls. I know all this—I'm not insane—yet there are times, these late-night hours, when I'm so filled with desire to feel alive again that I think I'm still sixteen and exploring Paris. I found Fitzgerald's apartment house near the Arc de Triomphe, a gray stone building that looked like a prison. I sat beneath the statue of Marshal Ney, then walked to Hemingway's apartment on Rue Notre-Dame-des-Champs, Gertrude Stein's apartment in a stippled courtyard of pigeons and ivy, Sylvia Beach's bookstore on Rue de l'Odéon. The sweet smells of exhaust and perfume met in the crowded cafés. American kids played their guitars by the fountains, hoping some generous Parisians would drop money into their upturned hats. Music poured from the radios on the Place Pigalle. Two wrestlers flexed and grinned, one of them spitting at the crowd. A woman holding the bottom of a torn paper bag stepped from the curb, just as, across the street, another woman walked through the back door of a striptease joint. An old man wearing rouge and a rose in his lapel followed me across Montmartre. A whore approached, smiling, and when I hesitated she ran her fingers up the inside of my thigh. Darkness turned Paris into a necklace of stars. "Nothing ever happens," Rebecca complained. "Nothing, nothing." Waiters skated through the cafés, trays held high. Blue shadows slid past like automobiles. Alice carefully maneuvered Rebecca between us, then changed her mind, laughing nervously, and skipped to my side, pretending she wanted to look at the watches in a store window. Timmy tagged along, mournfully attentive. In the garden outside the apartment, Alice brushed my arm and said, "Scobie has a secret to tell me." Rebecca lowered her eyes, slowly opened the door, and stepped inside. Timmy followed. I looked at Alice.

"I wanted a chance to talk," she said.

"About what?"

"We've avoided each other all summer. All our *lives*." She spoke into my eyes, watching for something. "Now that Larry's gone I thought . . ."

She shrugged, glancing toward the street. Perhaps it was the gesture, so abstracted and genuine, or perhaps it was the deep relief darkness cast, but I saw us both as we might have appeared to someone peering out the window, two dim shapes leaning toward each other, almost touching. That was *me*. Her hands reached uncertainly for my face and pulled me down to her soft warm lips. I could hear her heart beating between us. Strands of her hair, salty as the ocean, caught in my mouth. Our tongues touched. For a moment everything stopped moving, I felt the forces of our lives coming together after years of waiting, unknown to me, for this simple kiss. Suddenly spokes of light wheeled through the slats of the fence, startling as the slam of a door in an empty house. We jumped guiltily apart. Behind her I saw pools of light on the tile roofs, the feathered, silver trees.

"We should go in," she said.

I kissed her knuckles, the smooth dry palms of her hands.

"I love you," she said. "I always have." She raised her eyes and kissed my chin. "But you live on the moon, Scobie."

"No, I'm here."

"Are you?"

"Yes," I said. "Yes, I am."

I Know Your Heart,
Marco Polo

HASHID had tried to illustrate his point by telling Sam the story of a man who fell asleep, dreamed he was a butterfly, and, when he awoke, could not remember if he was a man who had dreamed he was a butterfly or a butterfly dreaming it was a man. As usual with Hashid, the connection between logic and metaphor remained vague. The story, however, Sam had understood, and as he walked back to work after lunch it seemed a truth that challenged his life. If he could not know which reality he should use to evaluate appearances, how could he ever make a decision? If he could not make decisions, he could not work. If he could not work, his family would starve. He sighed, shaking his head, switching his briefcase to his other hand and stopping to stare through the window of a travel agency. There, encased in afternoon light, hovered a miniature 727. Inside, people ate from plastic trays, laughed with the stewardesses, watched the movie. The details, though not the best, were good. Sam should know. He had spent weeks of his life on such airplanes. Tomorrow, in fact, he was supposed to fly to Washington, and the thought, like Hashid's story, upset him—not so much the thought of wasted hours in Washington as the thought of visiting his parents on Long Island. He looked at the poster of blond Amazons running into the sea as if it were an orgy. I've got to stop drinking coffee, he thought, turning back to the street. His stomach burned. A woman in a green miniskirt bumped against his shoulder, apologized in Persian, hurried away. She could have been a secretary walking to work in Hartford or New Haven. There was nothing except her voice to suggest she was not American. How long, he wondered, before the whole world looks like Hartford? Thirteen years ago, stepping off the airplane into Baghdad's blinding summer heat, he had felt like an explorer. Today, in Teheran, he felt like a traveling executive. Everyone spoke English. Rooms were air-conditioned. But there were still some mysteries left: Persepolis, Shiraz. Sam crossed the street, walked through the compound gates and across the lawn. He opened the embassy door.

Charlie, the Marine guard on duty, rose and nodded. "Good afternoon, sir."

"Good afternoon, Charlie."

Charlie looked like one of the statues Sam had seen last summer on the shore of the Caspian, statues of the first Aryans, tall and wide-shouldered, proud as veterans saluting the flag. Had he been trained to stand so straight, smile so innocently? Sam walked past the bulletin boards and water coolers to his office. *Deputy Chief of Mission,* read a brass plaque on his door.

Sue Benson was sipping coffee and squinting at her typewriter. "Hi, Sam. This damn thing's broken again."

"Call the C.I.A.," he said, walking into a large room with a bookshelf in the corner and a gray metal desk by the window. Some of the framed miniature paintings he collected were hanging on the white walls. The light was dim, almost green, diffused by the shutters covering the windows. He sat down at his desk. Sue brought him a cup of coffee. Her brown hair, cut short and tinted blond, swayed before her blue eyes. She brushed it away, smiling. Sam could not look at her.

He lit a cigarette. "Is the typewriter really broken?"

"Kaput," she said. "I'll get Jimmy to fix it. Oh, and you're supposed to see Ambassador Anderson."

"When?"

"Now."

"What about?"

"I don't know."

"Anything else?"

"No. Yes." She stopped in the doorway. "It's your anniversary today."

"Christ. Thank you."

Sam watched his cigarette smoke spin slowly toward the ceiling. How long had he been married to Laura? He sat back and counted the years. Twenty-seven. Impossible. He counted again. Yes, twenty-seven. He would soon be fifty. That too seemed impossible. Stubbing out his cigarette, he looked at the papers on his desk. He could not concentrate. He kept thinking about Sue. She had been his secretary, off and on, for fifteen years. Last night, after working late, he had driven her home and, several drinks later, led her to bed and undressed her. It was the first time he had been unfaithful to Laura. This fact alone, he suspected, should have stupefied him. The memory of Sue's apartment, its efficient, lonely simplicity—white shag rug, glass-topped table, empty flower vases—depressed him. She had spent half her life devoted to her job, yet she did not, like most secretaries, exude a crisp dry disdain for any passion except patriotism. He had seen her dating junior officers, Marine guards. They took her out to dinner or bowling at the Army club. She must have slept with some of them. Sam had not paid much attention before, to her or any other woman. Sex should be shared, like fear, between husband and wife. Sex was embarrassing unless it was not just sex. Then why, so late, had he wanted to sleep with Sue? It was stupid, self-destructive. He wished he knew himself better. Did he love her? His stomach turned over, sluggishly, like a dying engine. He imagined leaving Laura and felt he had killed her. Memory took her place. Something like passion, anguish, immediately stirred in him again, and he wanted her back. He stood abruptly, picked up his briefcase, and left his office.

Sue looked up and smiled. "Good luck."

He bent across her desk and kissed her. She tasted of toothpaste and coffee.

"You mustn't forget Quentin," Laura said, staring out from the terrace to the swimming pool, where he and Matthew were lying in the sun. "He's so looked forward to your coming."

"I haven't forgotten him," Scobie said.

"You know what I mean. He wants to do things with you."

"Mom, he's only sixteen."

"And you're so old you can't remember what it was like to be sixteen?"

"No, I haven't forgotten."

"All right. Just be considerate, that's all. Promise?"

The heat pressing down through the striped awning above her head made Laura feel drowsy, thick-limbed. She sipped her iced tea and glanced at Scobie. The mustache he had started growing a few summers earlier had thickened and spread into a full beard and his long hair rose from his head in a chaotic cluster of curls. He was wearing blue-jeans, a faded blue shirt, and blue espadrilles. Did he think that after graduating from college he could continue to wear such clothes? "Scobie, tell me, what have you decided to write your thesis on?"

"Fitzgerald." He picked up his cigarette. "Do you know that when Fitzgerald was writing *The Great Gatsby* he lived near Nana and Pa?"

"Yes."

"You did?"

"Yes."

"Mother, you're full of surprises. One of these days, I'm going to find that house."

The soccer stadium across the street erupted with clapping and whistling. Someone had just scored a goal.

"Time for my nap," Laura said, standing. "What are you going to do this afternoon?"

"I don't know. Matthew and I were thinking of visiting Penelope."

"Penelope?"

"A girl we met on the airplane."

"Why don't you take Quentin with you?"

"We'll corrupt him, Mother. You have no idea what evil things we do when we're alone."

"I'd rather he were corrupted than lonely. So there. And don't forget, we're having people for dinner. Don't be late."

The front hallway was cool and dark, a long tiled room that ran back to the stairs. On either side, more rooms swirled in shadow, the coolness trapped by the closed shutters. Laura climbed the stairs to her bedroom, took off her clothes, and lay down on the sheets, feeling that she was someone else, or herself as she had once been, another woman lying beside her. She picked up *Messer Marco Polo* from the bedside table. Jenny Taylor had sent her the book, along with a letter saying her daughter Alice was soon to be married. Scobie had once been in love with Alice. Laura suspected that he was still in love with the memory of that first love, for when she told him he had seemed genuinely shocked. "Alice? Married?" Laura tried to read, but her mind was distracted by her sons laughing in the garden. The telephone rang. "Hello?"

"Laura?"

It was Nick Sinclair. The sound of his voice made Laura start to sweat under her arms. She could taste lunch at the back of her throat. "Hello, Nick."

"What are you doing?"

"Reading."

"I'd like to see you."

"Nick, I can't. I've got to get ready for this evening."

"Just half an hour or something. We could have tea."

"When?"

"Around four. Is that all right?"

"Where?"

"I don't know. The Hilton?"

"Okay."

"Good. I'll see you at four."

"Nick, why?"

"I need to talk, Laura. I just need to talk."

Sam sat down next to Nick at the Ambassador's long mahogany table.

"Good afternoon," Pericles said.

He was about sixty, a bachelor, dressed in his usual synthetic gray suit and drip-dry shirt. A thick silver watch glinted on his freckled wrist. He was from Texas, a poor boy who had lived in a chicken coop during the Depression. Somehow, since then, he had made several million dollars in oil and real estate. Nixon had appointed him ambassador a week after the last election—one year ago. Sam and Nick once spent an entire lunch hour trying to guess how he had come by his name. Nick was wearing a seersucker suit and cotton shirt. His hair was red, and he spoke in a slow, measured voice that irritated Pericles because it sounded so condescending. Nick's background—Andover and Harvard—had never entirely disappeared.

"So what's the story on this heroin business?" Pericles asked.

"The general is a seller," Nick said.

"Are you sure?"

"I'm sure."

"Can you prove it?"

"No. Not yet."

"Anyone else?"

"Sure. A few bankers. A minister or two. The oil people. And someone else, someone even bigger. I don't know who."

"Yet," Sam said. "But you will. Soon. Right?"

Nick shrugged. "Maybe."

"We can only pressure them," Pericles said, clenching his small, fat hand on the table. "Tell them we know and remind them of our arms aid, technical advice, and so on down the line."

Nick looked out the window, as if the proper response were floating in sunlight. "That won't do any good. I'm telling you, everyone's involved. Right up to the top. A defense contract is nothing compared to what they can get selling heroin."

Through the window Sam saw the gardener idly watering the lawn with a glistening black hose. An airplane buzzed overhead. Perhaps someone, as the airplane banked to climb still higher, was looking through his round window at the roof of the embassy. The city was silent, though the jails were crowded with students, poets, beggars, assassins, though the walls of the jails beat like hearts. Perhaps a poet was reading aloud in the darkness of his cell. Perhaps the other prisoners were listening, trying to remember why they were prisoners. Perhaps, outside the city, on the shore of a field, Hashid's father watched his grandchildren playing. Could he hear their piercing laughter? Behind them, did the tall trees wave their dark green branches in the air? Did the complicated, co-ordinated shifting of shadows remind him of troops assembling in the desert? Perhaps he knew he would die before he completed his memoirs. History, his own life, had vanished. He knew it made no difference. He listened to his grandchildren. They sounded like birds. A truck backfired in the street. Sam jumped.

"Well, try," Pericles was saying. "It's our only hope."

"We can't touch them?" Nick asked.

"No." Pericles shook his head. "Regrettably."

Sam had already been posted to Greece, Iraq, Jordan, Kuwait, and Egypt, but counting the countries did not convince him he had been there. Hashid was right. Dreams within dreams. What would happen to Hashid? A modest, intelligent man, a collector of Persian miniatures, husband and father—he could have been Sam. Powerless to use his knowledge about heroin trafficking, he had passed the information on to Nick, and now Nick too found himself powerless to use it. Failures within failures. Sam tried to listen to Pericles but his mind wandered to Laura, to Sue, to Scobie, Matthew, Quentin. It was summer vacation for his sons, a time to watch your father and mother try to be the parents they were when you were young and they took you to the beach. Maybe his sons would end up on the moon. It did not seem possible, yet it might happen. An impossible possibility. He hated that kind of paradox, but it was one of the things, part of the age, he had learned to appease with benign neglect.

"I'll see you both tonight." Pericles stood.

The meeting was apparently over.

Outside, in the corridor, Nick touched Sam's arm and said, "One of these days, I'm going to quit." He was serious, his gray eyes angry.

"No, you won't," Sam said. "You're hooked. Just like me. What does Hashid say?"

"Nothing. He's scared."

"I don't blame him."

"Nor do I. If I were he, I'd disappear."

"So would I," Sam said.

From his bedroom window at the back of the house Quentin could see rows of artichokes reaching to the garden wall. Though he was too old to play with toy soldiers any more, the orderly beauty of imaginary wars continued to hold him. And his coins, worn thin as wafers by centuries of handling, would have told him, if only they could speak, what had really happened in history. Neither soldiers nor coins, however, could lift his present boredom. He sat down on his bed, leaned back against the white wall, and stared through the window at the bare patch of Persian sky, pale and smooth as porcelain. Matthew had gone to see Penelope. Scobie was in his room, writing. Boredom's the wrong word, Quentin decided, lighting a forbidden cigarette and using an empty silver film container for an ashtray. I'm not bored. I'm frustrated. He knew what he wanted to do, he wanted to go to college, like Matthew and Scobie. Whatever they were doing there, it was more exciting than high school. Both his brothers had changed so much in the past few years. They reminded Quentin of soldiers home from battle. Even their pain was exclusive. He heard the door to his parents' room opening. Pushing out his cigarette, he dropped the butt into the container, screwed on the silver top, and carefully hid the cylinder in his desk drawer. His own door was ajar. He saw his mother crossing the hallway toward the stairs. Something about the way she walked reminded him of someone. Himself, he realized. She was practically tiptoeing, furtive. Why? Where was she going? He waited until she had descended the stairs, then moved quickly to her study, a small room with a window overlooking the front garden, the swimming pool. He saw her hurrying across the garden and into the car, driving out through the gate, and disappearing down the street. The sight of the vanishing black Mercedes filled him with sadness.

"What's up?"

Quentin turned and saw Scobie standing in the doorway.

"Just looking," he said.

"At what?" Scobie asked.

"Mom."

Scobie peered through the window. "Where?"

"She's gone. In the car."

"So?"

"She was acting funny."

"She's a funny person."

"No, I mean strange."

"She's a strange person."

"I think she's having an affair."

"Oh, come on, Quentin. Mother? An affair?"

"I've seen her sneaking out a lot recently."

"She's probably going to see her guru."

"I don't think so."

"Or shopping. Or visiting friends. Or driving around in circles."

"She acts like a kid sneaking out to smoke a cigarette."

Scobie laughed. "Sherlock Richardson on the job. An affair, huh?"

"Do you think it's possible?" Quentin asked.

"I don't know. Sure, I guess it's possible. Everyone else has affairs. Why shouldn't our mother? On the other hand, you have a very active imagination. And I'm very suggestible. Let's go swimming."

Quentin returned to his room and put on his bathing suit. Scobie was waiting for him in the cool hallway. They walked down the stairs together. A fan turned slowly overhead. Outside, the sun was so bright Quentin had to squint. The garden lost its separate parts, became one color, one sound, one smell, not filtered and refined by his consciousness but absorbed by his body. A truck backfired in the street, the garden spun inward to shape, and he stepped off the terrace, across the grass, and dove into the pool. Cold water slapped him like a hand. As he surfaced he felt the concussion of Scobie's dive behind him. The water rippled, slapped the side of the pool, and Scobie exploded in light. They hovered together, listening to the birds, the cars on the street beyond the high wall, the children in the garden next door. Looking up at the house, Quentin saw the window of his mother's study, the ghost of his own face staring down at the pool.

"Remember that game we used to play at the Taylors'?" Scobie asked. "Marco Polo. Do you remember?"

"Yes."

"Let's play. You're it."

Quentin closed his eyes and listened. He heard Scobie swimming to the other end of the pool. "Marco," Quentin said.

"Polo," Scobie replied, diving.

Quentin waited, listening. Then, to his left, he heard Scobie gasping and giggling. "Marco," Quentin called.

"Polo," Scobie said.

Quentin dove, his eyes still closed, toward the sound of Scobie's voice. He could feel Scobie swimming above him, twisted, reached for what he hoped would be an ankle, and came up empty-handed. "Marco!"

"Polo!"

Hearing Scobie inhale and dive, Quentin dropped straight down, his arms spread wide, and caught his brother by the shoulder. They both surfaced, laughing.

Hashid was waiting for Sam and Nick at a crowded coffee house inside the bazaar. They sat down next to him at a round brass table and accepted small white cups of sweet Turkish coffee. Hashid was a Muslim, and received all friends, even unknown guests, with a gentle, cere-monious courtesy that made Sam feel slightly obese. This afternoon, Hashid was silent, watching with melancholy eyes as they sipped their coffee, his dark, smooth hands cra-dling his own cup as if it were a bird's egg filled with fragile life. Finally he spoke. "Ambassador Anderson?"

Nick nodded. "We saw him. His orders are to lay off."

"You cannot interfere?"

"No."

"Investigate?"

"That wasn't mentioned." Nick smiled.

Hashid sadly shook his head and stared into his coffee. "We can do nothing."

"We can do a great deal," Nick said. "We have to be careful, that's all. Especially you, Hashid."

"What can I do?" Hashid lifted his hands, a frustrated shrug.

"Continue to gather information and pass it along to me." Nick's voice was a soft and soothing monotone. "And help me find some people to infiltrate. Low level. Runners. It doesn't matter. We need someone closer, someone who might see a face or hear a name."

"Perhaps."

"Slowly, Hashid. That's the only way. Slowly and carefully."

"I'll try."

"Look, our problem is simple," Nick said, folding his hands on the table. "Either we lay off or pursue the issue more or less on our own. What do you want to do?"

"Go ahead," Hashid said firmly.

"So do I," Nick said. "Sam?"

"Privately, you know I'm with you, Nick. But I can't have anything more to do with the operation. If I did, I'd have to lie to the Ambassador."

"Fine."

Hashid spread his arms and smiled. "You are good men."

Nick grinned.

"Well, I must leave you now." Standing, Hashid shook their hands. "I'm flying to Isfahan."

"Business?"

"Always. Goodbye. Thank you."

Sam watched Hashid's lithe body disappear into the crowd.

Nick ordered more coffee. "He's taking chances."

"I know," Sam said. "Would you do what he's doing?"

"Yes."

Sam stared into the bazaar's twisting, penumbral alleys. They looked like rivers flowing toward darkness. On the cluttered shores men in white kafias offered their wares: brass bells, carpets, spices and olivewood boxes inlaid with ivory, coins, fruit, clothes, knives, clocks. High above the squatting, chattering hawkers and the oblique, curious glances of the customers, light penetrated holes in the black goatskins stretched across the top of the bazaar. Nick leaned toward Sam. "Ready?"

"You go on without me," Sam said. "I've got to try and find an anniversary present for Laura."

"Oh." Nick looked down at his hands. "Okay. See you later."

He stepped lightly from the café, his seersucker suit vanishing into the darkness. Sam took a swallow of his coffee and grimaced. It was cold. He looked at his watch. Three-thirty. As he stood to leave, he felt a hand on his arm, turned, and saw a peeling face. It was a beggar, dressed in blue, his fingers plucking at Sam's sleeve. Sam quickly gave him some money and hurried away.

Penelope sat by the edge of her swimming pool, her ankles dangling in the water, her body leaning back on her hands, her face lifted up to the sun. Matthew called her

name. She did not respond. He considered tapping her
shoulder, but that seemed absurd, so he imagined he was
on the terrace at home, with his mother, listening to the
shouts in the stadium across the street. Penelope smiled, her
eyes closed, helpless before the severity of his need, the in-
tensity with which he could, for a moment, desire her. She
was not stupid, but he knew he could, if he wished, convince her that even his lust would make her happy. She
started talking about her college boyfriend. They had lived
together for two years. "Then I got pregnant," she said. "I
didn't want an abortion, Bob didn't want me to have an
abortion, so I had a baby, a girl, and now I've got stretch
marks—no, don't look. That's why I don't take off my
shirt. I gave my baby away, Matthew. Can you imagine? To
a complete stranger. Our relationship immediately disin-
tegrated. Bob's and mine, I mean. There was something
about giving our baby away that killed our love. It made us
hard inside. We used to lie together in bed, not touching.
He'd tell me, 'Your breasts are beautiful.' But he never
touched me. The son of a bitch. Matthew, it would make
you sick to see my stretch marks. They're like scars."

She turned on the radio, her blunt fingers fiddling with
the plastic dial, a sweep of her red hair hiding her eyes,
her whole body bent, supplicant, before the invisible singer.
Matthew climbed out of the pool and approached her, his
feet leaving a path of evaporating footprints behind him.

"Do you ever dream of a perfectly happy life?" she
asked, lighting a cigarette so awkwardly he realized she was
safe, his own guilt made her invulnerable.

"Yes." He sat down next to her on the hot cement.

"Why do we do that? It's so *dumb*."

Matthew laughed. "Would you like to take some acid?"

She sat up and looked at him. "You have some? Here?"
"Yes."

"Wow." She glanced down, nervously, at her bitten fingernails.

He stared at her soft skin, her freckles, her green eyes, her hair so red it seemed to be burning. Why did girls with red hair always bite their fingernails?

"Okay," she said. "I haven't tripped since Bob and I broke up."

"Let's not if you don't want to."

"No, no, I want to," she insisted.

"You know, I can't stay much longer. I have to get back. Mom's having people for dinner. Maybe we should wait until we have more time."

"No, I'd like to trip now."

"Okay." Matthew reached into the pocket of his carefully folded bluejeans and pulled out a plastic bag. From the bag he pulled two pink pills. He handed one to Penelope.

"I'll get some water," she said.

"I'll come with you."

Following her toward the house, he saw himself in the plate-glass window growing larger, approaching himself. Penelope slid back the glass door and they stepped into a dim, carpeted living room chilly with air-conditioning. She poured two glasses of iced tea in the kitchen and they swallowed their pills.

"Want to hear some music?" she asked.

"Sure."

She searched through the albums piled on the living room floor, picked one, and put it on a stereo hidden inside the squat Spanish cabinet. Matthew sat down cross-legged. Penelope stretched out next to him, her wrist covering her eyes, and sang along with the music. Beautiful rock-and-roll, Matthew thought. He could chart his life with rock-and-roll: the slow dance of childhood, the anxious, pantomimed jitterbug of adolescence. The first rock-and-roll he remembered was an Elvis Presley song Scobie's friend Larry used to sing, accompanying himself on an old guitar. " 'Don't be cruel, to a heart that's true.' " Whatever happened to Larry?

"Shit," Penelope muttered.

"What?"

"I left my cigarettes outside."

Neither of them moved.

"Are you going to the fireworks tonight?" Matthew asked.

"Yes."

"Me, too. Maybe I'll see you there."

"That would be nice."

"Have you started to get a buzz yet?"

"I think so. Have you?"

"Yeah, a little. What's the record?"

"I don't know." Penelope giggled. "I can't remember."

Stepping off the hot street into the garden, Sam relaxed, he breathed deeply. He felt he was home. Trees and flowers surrounded the small swimming pool. Next door, beyond the high wall, children were playing beneath the pines. Shouts and applause, a deep, rumbling murmur, floated from the soccer stadium and across the garden. He walked upstairs to the cool, still bedroom, took off his clothes, and lay down for an hour. Laura was in the kitchen giving last-minute dinner instructions to the cook. Or she was sitting in her small room off the hallway, wearing a bathrobe, sipping tea and writing in her journal. The noise of the city receded behind the garden wall. Sam rose and showered. Dressing for dinner, he stared at his face in the mirror. It looked gray, ashen, dry as paper. He had not taken a vacation in years. His body had started to sag toward his belly. I should retire, he thought. Get out while I'm still capable of doing something. He had seen too many friends retire to fear and uselessness. They had waited too long, hoping for a final glory, one last important assignment. They didn't know what else to do, where to go, why. Sam carefully knotted his tie, feeling himself twenty-eight years earlier also knotting his tie as he prepared to meet Laura for dinner and ask her to marry him. Twenty-eight years. With half his heart he wanted to leave Laura, start over, feel some passion in his life again. Sue desired him, that was the difference between her and Laura, and he desired Sue intensely, the release he had shared with her last night. Dark spots of sweat dampened his clean white shirt. He turned away from the mirror, pulling his green-and-black checked jacket from the closet and walking into the bedroom. Laura was sitting on the bed, in her slip, reading. She was so absorbed she did not hear him enter the room. He stood and watched her. My life, he thought. He could not even remember falling in love with her. Hashid really was right. You wake from one dream into another. A sense of grace, what Sam called beauty, was all that existed to suggest reality. He had stopped painting seriously the day he realized he did not have the talent to capture it, reveal it. But maybe he should try again. Maybe he gave up too easily. "Laura?"

She looked up from her book. "Hello, darling. Am I late? Sam, what's wrong?"

"Nothing. Tired."

"You're pale as a ghost."

"Can't a man feel tired?"

"There's no need to use that tone of voice with me, Sam Richardson." She closed her book, stood, walked to her closet. "We've all got problems."

"What are your problems?" he asked.

"At the moment, you." Her back was to him as she searched for a dress. "You're freaked out, as the boys would say. You're frightened and you won't admit it."

"Goddamn it, Laura, you're talking like your goddamn guru."

"You've never met my goddamn guru."

"I'm going to get a drink. Want one?"

"We never even fight any more."

He stopped in the doorway. "What did you say?"

"I said, 'We never even fight any more.' " She was facing him now, boldly.

"Jesus Christ, woman, if we fought I'd leave you bleeding."

He almost ran down the stairs. The front door was open and he could see the setting sun reflected in the swimming pool. He walked into his study and mixed himself a Martini, sat down at the desk, and peered at his half-finished model airplane. He lit a cigarette. He rose and strode across the hallway, into the blue living room. Everywhere he went, twilight crept with him. He walked from lamp to lamp, leaving behind a string of soft lights. He drew the curtains. He sat down on the long couch. His marriage was a house. If he started exploring, he would discover, in each room, a year of his life. In the last room, he would find himself curled in a film of silence, water, heartbeat. He sipped his drink. Perhaps he was tired. Maybe all he needed was a rest. If he retired, he could paint again.

The doorbell rang. The arrival of the guests, their belief in him, made him believe in himself, and he stood from the couch to greet them.

As Scobie changed he could hear his parents arguing in their bedroom. He closed his door and looked in the mirror. Should he shave off his beard? No, he decided, though he often resented both his beard and long hair and wished he could shed this messy, graceless uniform. He put on a clean white shirt and a clean pair of bluejeans, then pulled a small wooden box, a slender pipe, and a letter from his suitcase. Matthew had not returned from Penelope's yet. The room was peaceful, early evening light filtering in through the window. Below, in the garden, the swimming pool was as still as the mirror. Scobie sat down in a chair by the window, opened the box, crumpled a chunk of hashish into the pipe, and smoked, his feet up on the windowsill. Opening the letter, he read it for the third time. It was from Susan, who was spending the summer in New York, working for Welfare. Her letters were written in a funny, Victorian syntax that made him ache to be with her. He remembered her small smells—perfume, wool, sweat, apprehension—and nearly moaned. Why was he spending the summer at home when he could have stayed with her? I must be crazy, he thought. What if I get back and she doesn't love me any more? There was a knock on the door. "Who is it?"

"Quentin."

"Come in."

His brother walked into the room, dressed for dinner, his eyes shyly circling the room, then resting on Scobie. "What're you doing?"

"Uh, reading."

"What's that smell?"

Scobie laughed. "Dope. Hash. Want some?"

"I don't know," Quentin said, sitting down on the bed nearest the window. "I've never tried it."

"Want to?"

Quentin hesitated. "Yes."

"Maybe you're too young," Scobie said. "Maybe I'm corrupting you. But what the hell. This is great stuff. Afghan. I'll just break a bit off, like so, and then light my trusty match. Quentin, don't worry about it. It's not going to hurt you. Really. Okay?"

"Yeah."

"All right. If I can just get this damn match . . . okay. Now, slowly, that's it—no, too much." Scobie slapped his gagging brother on the back. "Okay?"

"Yeah," Quentin gasped.

"Want to try again?"

"Yeah."

"Now, slowly. Perfect, beautiful. Enough, don't be greedy, keep it in, very good. Now, slowly, let it out. Okay?"

"Yeah." Quentin smiled.

"Next time, hold it in a little longer. How're you feeling?"

"Yeah. I mean, fine."

Scobie lit the pipe a few more times and they passed it between them. Then they both sat back and stared at each other, Scobie already forgetting the evening he sat by the window, the way the air reflected the city's tired collapse, the distant clamor of horns and screeching brakes. Instead, he was a child again, waiting with Alice Taylor for the bus to take them to school. As he waited, he tried to memorize a poem: " 'The highwayman came riding, riding, up to the old inn door.' "

"Haven't you learned that yet?" Alice exclaimed.

"Of course," he said. "I'm just practicing."

Meanwhile, in his head, highwaymen and galleons, moonlight and shutters, cobblestones and dead daughters all whirled together in absolute confusion, a beautiful chaos he was sure he would never master. Alice stood so close he could have caressed her cheeks. Her small fingers clasped her satchel, her hair rose toward him like golden seaweed. The bus arrived, doors hissing open, and they were pulled inside by heat. Hands reached down from straw baskets, briefcases, and packages of patterned paper, steering them through the sweet smells of bread and perfume to a seat by a window, where they sat and watched the passing awnings, waving trees. The bus ride seemed to last forever. They grew older, watching the world through the window. Alice held his hand, seriously, comfortably. They knew each other so well their own children might know themselves in their tranquility. She smiled, seeing something in the street that pleased her. They never left the bus, they never moved from their seats, their childhood marriage. So why was she skipping across the gravel schoolyard, her satchel slapping her thigh, her yellow dress a spot of sunlight beneath the pines, her voice calling back through the years, "Open the window, open the window!"

Sam watched his sons walk into the living room. They were smiling, almost giggling, Quentin obviously pleased to have his brothers home, Scobie and Matthew looking like ancient warriors, their hair so long it covered their shoulders. Sam handed Pericles a Martini. Pericles stiffened and blushed when he saw Scobie and Matthew. He thought they were hippies. Scobie waved. "Good evening, Mr. Ambassador. How goes the war machine?" Matthew laughed. Scobie shook hands with Pericles, looked at Sam. Behind his eyes, Sam saw himself staring back. He smiled. "Ambassador Anderson could have you deported for insolence."

Scobie laughed, touching Sam's arm. "Am I ruining your career?"

"What career? Want a drink?"

"Please. Gin and tonic. Good evening, Mr. Nightingale."

"Good evening, good evening." David Nightingale, a lecturer at the university, smiled apologetically, waved his words away, dismissed them. His hands hovered, uncertain birds, then fluttered into his pockets. His face was narrow and ascetically rugged—he seemed to have weathered many intellectual battles. This combination of incapacity and victory made him handsome.

"How's the world of literature?" Scobie asked.

"Terrible," David replied.

Scobie shook hands with Nick and Anne. Ice cubes clattered into a glass. "Thanks, Dad."

Sue was sitting on the arm of the couch, across the living room, talking to Laura. Sam watched them both. Younger than Laura, Sue was not as beautiful. Her plain, angular face, the awkward gestures she made with her long, pale hands, even her conservative clothes made Sam want to protect her. Laura laughed, resting her hands on Sue's arm. They leaned together like conspirators. Sam mixed drinks for Matthew and Quentin, then wandered over to talk to Nick. Anne left them alone, joining David and Pericles by the open window. Sam felt he was participating in an elaborate and very formal dance. Nick lit a cigarette and leaned back in his chair. He had the best mind Sam knew—quick, comprehensive, logical. Nick believed details were the truth, and looked for answers where others saw only incidentals. Years ago, when he and Sam were at Harvard, he had predicted, in his quiet way, that he would do something important and anonymous. Looking at him now, Sam realized how much he had aged. His red hair was graying. Light sparkled from his pink-framed glasses as he turned to Sam. "Your sons are stoned."

"What?"

"Stoned. Drugs."

"How do you know?"

"Because that's my son's natural state."

Sam stared across the room at Scobie, Matthew, and Quentin. They were sitting together, whispering and laughing. Scobie met his eyes and smiled self-consciously. Sam suddenly felt light-headed himself. "Is it like being drunk, I wonder?"

"Probably," Nick said. "Though they never make such fools of themselves as we do when we're drunk."

Sam shook his head. "Crazy times."

"Amen."

"Now they're putting a man on the moon."

Nick sipped his drink. "I remember reading Tom Swift and thinking, No one can fly to the moon. Impossible. Science fiction."

"You'd have to be insane to be one of those astronauts."

"No," Nick said. "Just too dumb to get scared."

Laughing, Sam watched Laura leave Sue and disappear into the kitchen. Immediately, Scobie sat down next to Sue.

She was flattered, flustered. Stoned or not, Scobie entertained. Sue was sexy, Sam admitted to himself.

"Laura told me you're going to Washington tomorrow," Nick said.

"That's right."

"They'll probably tell you to hold me back."

"Probably. On the other hand, they don't really know what you're doing."

"True." Nick pushed out his cigarette. "I don't envy you, though. I hate Washington."

Sam looked at him. "Do you realize you and I haven't lived in the country we're supposed to represent for over ten years? Not really *lived* there. I go back home and it's a foreign country. Yet we talk to foreigners as if we were Americans, as if there were some connection between what we do and what people are doing at home. That's even crazier than goddamn astronauts."

"You're getting cynical, Sam."

"Not cynical. Tired. Aren't you?"

"Sure I'm tired. And you know what else? The higher you get in this business, the more boring the job. All day long I sit at a desk shuffling papers. What the hell kind of job is that?"

"But you'll never quit."

"I'll have to, one of these days. They'll make me. Anyway, I'm getting tired of pushing around middle-aged failures."

"If you had it to do over, would you?" Sam asked.

"I don't know. I've had a good time."

"Me, too. As Laura reminds me, we've been very lucky."

"True." Nick pulled at his shirt collar, then ran his fingers down his silk tie. "Lucky and underpaid."

"Dinner," Laura announced from the doorway.

.   .   .

Passing the wine, Laura looked down the table at Nick's thinning red hair and handsomely broken nose, his large knuckles, his eyes—they varied, in different lights, from green to pale gray—swimming in the lenses of his glasses. For weeks, he and Laura had been meeting at places like the Hilton bar, where he quietly and sadly confessed that he thought Anne was sleeping with another man, someone in the French embassy. This afternoon, Laura had noticed a new tone in his voice, needful, almost desperate. "I love you," he had declared, not knowing whether to smile or not. She told him he was confusing confession and love. "Perhaps," he conceded. But she knew she was attracted to Nick. She had been for years. He would always be the other possible man, the one with whom she would occasionally flirt, the one for whom she would dress, the one whose face would sometimes float through her mind as she held Sam in her arms. She had told Nick this, sitting in the dark Hilton bar, a shadowy world that seemed to revolve through the stripes of shadow and light cast by venetian blinds. Those few hours had both drained and filled her. To be wanted, to want, and yet remain untouchable—we torture ourselves, she thought. Nick's words, rising toward her in that aura of strained intimacy, had sounded as if they knew her, and she had not been able to explain to him that he did not know her, did not know the history of the other rooms she had shared with Sam.

"I have a friend who wouldn't speak for two months last semester," Scobie said. "He felt every word was a distortion, a manipulation of facts. He decided that to speak is to corrupt. So he was silent."

"Christ," Sam said, looking at Laura.

She looked away. What was Sam thinking? How much he desired Sue? She was young. She was lonely. She liked to make Sam happy. She had lovely legs and large breasts. They spent so much time together it would not be surprising if they loved each other. Laura's mind moved farther from the dinner table, the incomprehensible words filling the comfortable room. She remembered sitting on the porch every summer afternoon when she was a little girl, listening to her best friend Cassie practicing her cello next door. Laura could hear every note. Mrs. MacKenzie, stooped in her garden plucking lettuce, would stop and listen too, her eyes clouding like a sailor's. But now Laura was miles and years from that shady street, those summer afternoons. Now she was living a particular life in a particular way at a particular time, and no matter what she thought or dreamed or desired her path was marked and she was traveling on it toward a place that had been waiting for her since birth. She had sat by beds all night, watching dreaming children, their fragile bodies struggling not to drown, their hearts racing fear. What did Nick know about that? Down dark hallways, a caught breath can sound like a scream. Nick and I will be separated forever by all that we've never experienced together, she thought, trying to catch up with the conversation. They were talking about Matthew. "How is leaving college going to help?" she asked. "How can you solve anything by withdrawing, hiding?"

David and Laura laughed, sharing a secret. Sam put down his wine, his chest tightening, his tongue thick and dry. Were they having an affair? Could a limp-wristed professor of poetry, in patched tweeds and frayed woolen ties, steal his wife? Fear and sadness rose through Sam's body. He tried eating, but everything tasted of iron.

"Your father tells me you want to leave college," Pericles said to Matthew.

"Yes, sir."

"Why?"

"I'm not learning anything."

"Anything?"

"I'm not learning what I want to learn."

"And what would that be?" Sam asked.

"I told you, Dad, it's hard to talk about. It's hard to put into words."

"I have a friend who wouldn't speak for two months last semester," Scobie said. "He felt every word was a distortion, a manipulation of facts. He decided that to speak is to corrupt. So he was silent."

"Christ," Sam said. Laura smiled and looked away.

"What would you do?" Nick asked.

"Travel," Matthew said.

"Where?"

"It doesn't really matter. Afghanistan, maybe. Or India."

"You know, I really don't understand you guys," Sam said. "You act as if the world were falling apart."

"It is."

"Horseshit. Excuse me. Religious fanatics have been predicting our downfall for centuries. We're still here, aren't we?"

"For the time being, yes."

"How is leaving college going to help?" Laura asked. "How can you solve anything by withdrawing, hiding?"

"Mom, part of the problem is your faith in solving problems," Matthew said. "Every time we solve a problem, we create new problems. Each new problem is more difficult to solve than the last, more dangerous than the last. Vietnam is a solution to a problem created by another solution. Right?"

"You have to work, Matthew," Sam said.

"Not for the government."

"When I was your age, working for the government seemed an honorable thing to do. Should I grow my hair long and pick fleas in Vermont? Is that what I should do?"

"I didn't say that."

David cleared his throat. " 'And we are here as on a darkling plain swept with confused alarms of struggle and flight, where ignorant armies clash by night.' "

"Oh, shut up," Sam said.

"Sam."

He felt like a child. "I'm sorry."

"Let's not talk about politics any more," Laura said.

"You sound like Nana," Scobie said. "What else is there to talk about?"

"Living."

"What you call living is for the rest of the world a political problem."

"Intellectuals solve nothing," Pericles pronounced.

"I'm not an intellectual." Scobie laughed.

"What are you laughing about?" Sam said.

"Nothing."

Sam started to laugh too. "Nothing?"

"Nothing," Scobie said.

"I think you're both out of your minds," Laura said. "Somebody please tell me something nice."

"I have an announcement to make." Sam smiled. "Today is our anniversary. We've been married twenty-seven years."

He reached into his jacket pocket and passed Laura a small white box. She took the box, looking at him, amazed, and held it before her like an offering. Scobie and his brothers clapped, whistled, stamped their feet. Nick and Anne raised their glasses in a toast. Pericles grinned, despite himself, flushed and slightly drunk. David sang congratulations, his bitterness disguised as ceremony. Sue's eyes moistened. Opening the box, Laura removed a small golden bird. "Oh, Sam, it's beautiful."

"Over a thousand years old," he said. "The gift of some ancient emperor to his lovely princess."

He felt he was driving a knife through Sue's breasts, into her heart.

"Thank you," Laura said. "Thank you, thank you."

Quentin looked at his mother. She had lost weight, just as his father had gained weight, and he imagined the process continuing until she was thin air and his father pure matter. He felt he was looking at a photograph taken of her before he was born. Though her hair, cut short, was beginning to gray, and a few wrinkles creased the corners of her eyes, she seemed a young girl waiting for a date. She was not the woman he had always thought of as his mother but a stranger who had inadvertently become his mother—a vague double who filled the room with rage and delight. "Do you know why the flower is so important in Persian poetry?" she asked Ambassador Anderson. "Imagine spending days and days on the desert, then arriving in Isfahan or Shiraz. Imagine the trees, the gardens, the water. Imagine what a flower means to a man who lives on the desert."

"Don't forget the fireworks."

"We have half an hour. Plenty of time."

"I know it's silly, but I love watching fireworks," Sue said, immediately blushing.

Matthew and Ambassador Anderson started arguing about Vietnam. The words were always the same. Both his brothers, Quentin knew, were opposed to the war. They had marched in protest many times. Matthew had been arrested for throwing chicken blood at Senator Klee. Scobie said he was going to avoid the draft. The war had become, for them, an obsession, and they would forgive no one who did not agree with them. "It's very simple," Matthew was saying. "We're the neighborhood bully picking on the small kid. We try to justify it with all sorts of rhetoric, but in fact there's no good reason to be there. We're just getting our sick kicks, that's all. We won't even admit we're trying to build an empire. We're afraid of losing. We're afraid of being emasculated. We're so insecure about ourselves that we're incapable of compassion. It's disgusting."

"I'm not sure I understand your logic. Are we building an empire or are we simply depraved bullies?"

"Both."

"Would you feel better if we were only building an empire? If there were good reasons to be there?"

"No."

Quentin stopped listening. He looked at Scobie, who was watching Matthew, a mixture of pride and fear on his face. Quentin wished Scobie would look at him that way. And what was going on between his mother and father? The tension was palpable. They had been arguing about something before dinner. He had never seen them really fight before. Usually they just lost their tempers with each other, became irritated and melancholy. Why did he feel their anger was his fault? Maybe he was imagining the whole thing. I'm stoned, he thought, much the way he had recently thought, I'm not a virgin any more. He realized this and wondered when it would end, when he would stop getting initiated into different and more complicated states of consciousness. His mother stood from the table, smiling. "Time to celebrate," she said, moving from the dining room toward the hallway.

"Quentin." It was Scobie, leaning close and whispering. "How're you doing?"

"Okay."

"This is getting a little weird," Matthew whispered, appearing beside them.

His brothers surrounded him, almost linking arms, and led him into the hallway, where everyone else was waiting by the front door. Matthew's fingers, light as a breeze, brushed Quentin's, inevitably reassuring. What was he trying to say?

The embassy was dark, the tops of the trees swayed like sleeping elephants. Around the walls, the city droned: automobiles, lovers. A street of small booths ringed the running children. Lights and laughter echoed in the darkness, but Sam listened to another sound, watched another sight, something within the celebration that was not a celebration. Looking up, he saw the moon waiting in stillness. Suspended above the lawn was a screen, and on the screen, which was as dark as the night, giant astronauts whirled through space, their white helmets glowing in a hidden light. They seemed to float and spin just inches above the lawn. Fireworks tattooed the air. A girl strode through the crowd, her red hair reflecting the cascading sparks. "I'll be right back," he said to Laura, stepping into the crowd. He jumped to see above the crewcuts, hair curlers, sunhats. The girl was fifty yards away, standing at a booth with a rifle in her hand. Sam pushed through the children. "Excuse me, excuse me." He arrived at the booth just as the girl, with a sly, coy smile at the young man behind the counter, lifted the rifle to her shoulder and fired a round of perfect shots into the heart of a cardboard figure. The young man handed her a purple giraffe. She leaned forward, breathlessly, to accept her prize, her gift, and her fingers lingered, for a second, upon the fingers of the young man. Sam walked back to Laura. Why had he followed that girl? More fireworks exploded above his head. In the shattering light, he saw Laura's face, as smooth and peaceful as a face in sleep.

She smiled. "It's beautiful, in a way, don't you think?"

"The fall of Pompeii," Sam said.

Scobie, Matthew, and Quentin stood next to her, watching the fireworks, the movie, astounded as natives glimpsing an airplane for the first time. David had disappeared. Sue was pitching pennies at one of the booths. Nick was up in his office, checking cables, and Anne—Anne too had disappeared. Sam looked at the moon again. It seemed so tranquil. He wondered what it would be like to be an astronaut, floating in silence far above the distant green earth. Terrifying, or peaceful? Nearby, someone shouted, and he turned to see a tribe of strangers walking through the compound gates, dressed in bright colors, cotton and silk. The men had long hair and the women's breasts were bared to suckling children. People turned and stared. Who were they? Sam looked for Nick or Pericles. Realizing he was the only officer present, he walked toward the tribe. When he reached the first man, he stopped. "Good evening," he said. "Who are you?"

"Reggie Castle. From Des Moines, Iowa. Pleased to meet you."

"What are you doing so far from home?" Sam asked, shaking Reggie's hand.

"We're in the Peace Corps."

"All of you?"

"Yes, sir."

"You're all Americans?"

"That's right. We've come for the Fourth of July."

"Okay," Sam said. "Welcome."

What else could he do? They worked for the government. They were Americans. They had as much right here as anyone else. He stood aside and smiled. They moved toward the movie, bracelets rattling and bells tinkling, sat down on the grass, cross-legged, and gaped at the spectacle.

"Amazing," Scobie said, coming up to Sam's side. "Who are they?"

"Peace Corps," Sam replied.

Scobie shook his head and laughed. "I don't believe this."

"What?"

"*This.*" He waved at the night. "That movie, the fireworks, the Army guys chugging beer, all those people in Bermuda shorts and madras shirts, and now . . . gypsies. It's incredible."

Sam walked away, through the embassy door to his office. Sue was sitting behind her desk, her face hidden in the palms of her hands. She did not look up. Sitting down, he listened to the firecrackers outside. Bursts of colored light pulsed in the dark room. "Sue?"

"Yes?" Her voice was muffled.

"What we did, last night?"

"Yes."

"We can't, ever again."

"I know." She raised her eyes and looked at him. "You didn't have to tell me that."

"Laura's my wife. She's the only woman I love. Oh, Christ, Sue, I want my marriage."

"I know, Sam."

"I'm sorry."

"Don't be." She straightened, looked through her purse for a handkerchief, and blew her nose. "Waste of time."

"If Laura knew—"

"Of *course* she knows." Sue leaned forward. "Sam, the pain is already there."

He was silent, watching the small explosions of light fill and darken her eyes. Fatigue, fluid and hot, rushed through his bones. Here I am, he thought. Aging diplomat, traveler and husband, father of three. His hands were sweating. He rubbed them dry on his thighs, loosened his tie. His chest, or heart, suddenly screamed. He bent forward and clasped his knees. Breathe slowly, he thought. Slowly, slowly. He needed one of his pills. They were at home in the drawer of the bedside table. Sue was leaning over him, her hands on his shoulders. The pain subsided, throbbed.

"Sam?" It was Nick, at the door. "We've got a problem. Better hurry."

Nick's voice, its sternness and conviction, pulled Sam from the chair, pulled his pain, like a hook, from his heart. "What's up?" he asked, following Nick down the corridor. "What's the matter?"

"Hippies," Nick said.

"What hippies? You mean the Peace Corps? What about them?"

"And soldiers."

"Hippies and soldiers?"

"Fight," Nick said. "Like cats and dogs, Americans and Russians."

They opened the embassy door and saw, in the careening light of the fireworks and the flickering, spectral movie, that the tribe had gathered in a circle. The women were in the middle, soothing their children. Soldiers jeered and threw beer cans from the periphery. Everyone else had surrounded the two groups and now stood watching, unmoving, mouths open. Nick and Sam hurried into the crowd and stepped between the Peace Corps and the soldiers. "All right, break it up," Sam said. He was furious, he realized. He wanted to knock heads together, hear the satisfying crunch of bone. "You," he said, pointing to one of the soldiers. "Move on. Beat it. What have these people done to you?" The soldier, obviously drunk, gave Sam the finger. Nick grabbed the soldier by the lapels and shook him. "You heard the man. Beat it." Another beer can sailed over their heads. A woman screamed.

"Out of the way, old man," a soldier said, pushing Sam aside.

Matthew paused to stare in the window of the travel agency at a miniature 727, convinced he could shrink and enter the airplane, fasten his seatbelt, and fly away. He had waited in hotels, airports, train stations, and bus terminals for the love of his life to walk by, swinging her long hair behind her and smelling of the ocean and summer. He might as well have been standing before a painting, hoping to will the woman brushing her hair by the window to turn and speak, shatter the heartbreaking light, touch him. He hurried after his brothers, through the compound gates. Two astronauts were floating and spinning above the black lawn. Matthew stopped and stared.

Scobie's fingers circled his arm. "I think I'm hallucinating. I see two giant astronauts over there."

"No, they're real," Quentin said. "I mean, it's a movie."

"What? A movie?" Scobie laughed. "But there's no plot, no message, nothing. We've been cheated. There's not even any sex. Or violence. Or catharsis, for Crissake. What would Aristotle say? He'd walk out. I'm walking out."

"Wait," Quentin said. "Look at the fireworks."

Hissing sparks sped streaking up, up, vanished, then suddenly reappeared, hesitant, concussive screams. Matthew saw the edges of trees, the clear, hard lines of the embassy, the stalls, booths, concessions, the bartering, playful soldiers. He looked at the stars, the moon—more words demanding sympathy. If only there were a way to slow the sentence, struggle without speaking. He felt the fireworks on his skin, the circles of light burning the backs of his eyelids. The muffled shuffling of feet reached him, a roar to accompany celestial detonations, people shouting at him to get out of the way so they could watch the mourners pass by, shaved and naked, stripped of teeth, watches, rings. Matthew stopped. Everyone, everywhere, stopped. Even the movie stopped, astronauts pinned to the screen. Then a Roman candle burst and everyone continued moving, slowly, as if he had never stopped but was mysteriously relaxed, almost happy. Matthew pressed the tips of his fingers to his closed eyes and saw a dark museum filled with trolley cars. Opening his eyes, he watched his hands sink back into his pockets. Don't slouch, he told himself, slouching. Why, he wondered, unexpectedly lucid, did the thought of leaving college seem so frightening? Was it because he would be leaving home as well, leaving forever the force that had always kept him and his brothers in the same orbit? Though he knew he must some day leave, he had thought the movement would be geographic, a simple matter of miles and hours. What if everyone left in every way? Was that already happening? He looked at his family's faces in the crackling light, then turned and stared at the movie screen, the swirling white astronauts, and remembered sitting with Scobie in a hot, dark room watching his first movie. There was no air inside the room, only breathing, the darkness, Scobie's hand, his familiarity suddenly threatened, a smell of men, and the swirling tunnel of light that became the movie. A deep stir rippled the darkness. Bodies heaved and settled. A man with gentle eyes was beaten and dragged. Small holes like screams were hammered into his hands. His body bled clouds that broke into rain as he slowly rose, his eyes looking down, forgiving Matthew, accusing Matthew. The darkness screamed, Matthew screamed, he screamed and screamed until his small body fell like a dead bird into Scobie's screaming hands. A ball of light rushed into the sky.

"A climbing comet," Scobie said, pointing. "They're showing the movie backward."

The light exploded into fragments, showering back down and extinguishing above the dark trees. Then another hissing rocket rose in a graceful arc toward the stars. This one exploded into red, white, and blue, a brief galaxy of color. Each rocket, when it exploded, shook the sky. Matthew wished he could draw a circle and step into it. The lawn trembled. The air smelled of sulfur. The embassy, the trees, the concession booths, the jerky figures of men and women glowed in the momentary illuminations, Penelope gliding through their midst, red hair tossed back, limbs friendly with the air—beauty's old self returned, radiant. Darkness again, moments of light, her face slipping away. Leaving his brothers, Matthew followed her, jumping from foot to foot to keep her in sight. He caught up with her just in time to see her accept a rifle from a blushing, smirking high school boy and fire a round of perfect shots into the heart of a cardboard figure. Fireworks splintered the sky. Bodies pressed their hot presence against him as he returned to his brothers. A stuttering voice called him to try his luck at pitching pennies. In times of peace, the militant man attacks himself. Why did he feel so betrayed? Had it started raining? He brushed the thought aside.

"I can't handle this," Scobie said. "Let's get out of here. Where's Mom?"

"She's already left," Quentin said.

"Okay. Let's go. Matthew?"

"Who'd you think you were?" Laura asked, stroking Sam's cheek with a hot washcloth. "Ben Hur? That you and Nick could take on the entire United States Army?"

"They started it," Sam muttered. He was sitting on the edge of the bed, naked, his head aching. "Anyway, nothing's broken. I'm okay."

"You're lucky."

"Lucky, hell. Bunch of ragdolls. No wonder we're losing in Vietnam."

Laura walked into the bathroom, squeezed the wash-cloth, and draped it over the sink. "Would you like any-thing?" she asked, returning to the bedroom.

"Yes," he said. "Champagne. It's our anniversary, after all. And the Fourth of July."

"Sam, are you sure you're not delirious?"

"Laura, champagne!"

She left the bedroom. He could hear her sandals slapping the tiles, the music on the Grundig downstairs. *"Lay lady lay, lay across my big brass bed."* He lit a cigarette. *"Stay lady stay, stay with your man a while."* The room, holding the light, held him too, close as the arms of sleep. He looked at the pictures on the walls, remembering all the bedrooms they had already seen. The bureau was from Baghdad, the chair from Egypt, the rug from Isfahan, the lamp from Athens. Laughter, warm and intimate, rose from the living room—his sons, each voice a subtle modulation of his own. Sweat slid down his arms. He was shaking. Pain pierced his chest again. He walked to the window and looked down at the dark trees, the silver swimming pool, the garden wall. For a moment, he stood spellbound, enchanted by something familiar, as if he had seen exactly the same garden in his childhood. Then he turned and looked back at the bedroom. He saw the order, the tran-quility, and was amazed. Did he live there? Returning to the bed, he sat down, closed his eyes, and leaned back against the pillow. The face of the soldier he had hit floated up, shocked and surprised. Sam wished he could fly to the moon, like one of those astronauts. He wished all he saw of life was the peaceful blue earth spinning in silence. But he knew he could only fly home and that the closest he would ever get to the moon would be his moth-

er's words: "Just think, dear, right this minute Laura and
the boys are probably watching the moon too." Laura appeared in the doorway, a bottle of champagne and two
glasses balanced on a copper tray. "Scobie opened it for
me," she said, nudging the door closed behind her and
resting the tray on the bedside table. Sam poured the
champagne. She took a glass and tried to smile.

"Laura, I'm sorry," he said.

"For what?"

"For what I've done."

"I believe you. I believe you're sorry. I believe you're un-
happy. But it's not just a question of what you've done. It's
not just Sue. Sam, what's happened to us?"

"Nothing," he said. "Nothing's changed."

"Sam, it's different now." She looked at him, sadness in
her eyes, sat down next to him on the bed, and held his
hand. "It's different now," she whispered. "There's nothing
to forgive."

"Laura?"

"Some part of me doesn't care, Sam. Some part of me is
dead. Isn't that awful? Oh, Sam, isn't that horrible?"

Scobie sat cross-legged on the living room floor with his
brothers, listening to Dylan and watching the moon
through the open window. Words and music floated from
the old Grundig, carrying Matthew's mind from fantasy to
fantasy, singing the secret life of all Quentin knew. Outside, city noises hummed, the lulling murmur of crickets
and cars. Despite the war, despite the riots, despite the
crazy loss of tranquility, Matthew realized he was happy,
tonight, sitting here with his brothers. There was nothing to

lose, nothing to leave behind. No one could take this moment from Scobie, no one could argue its existence. There it was, air and faith. Matthew, his hair held from his eyes by a red bandana, lay back on the floor and gazed at the ceiling. "Have either of you guys noticed something weird going on around here?" he asked, rolling over and staring at Scobie and Quentin. "Between Mom and Dad?"

"Yes."

"What?"

"They're having an argument," Scobie said.

"No, no, it's more than an argument."

"Quentin thinks Mother's having an affair."

"An *affair?* Mom?" Matthew was incredulous, almost mocking.

"Why not?" Quentin asked.

"She'd never do that," Matthew said.

"How do you know?" Scobie asked.

"I just know Mom, that's all. She really *believes* in her marriage. She'd never jeopardize it."

"Maybe." Scobie stared at Matthew. "I hope you're right."

"Why?" Quentin insisted. "What's wrong with Mom having an affair?"

"It's tacky."

"Everybody else's mother does. You said so yourself."

"Quentin, do you *want* Mom to be having an affair?" Matthew asked.

"Not particularly. But I don't think there's anything necessarily wrong with it. I don't see why we should get upset."

"Who's upset?" Scobie asked.

"You're upset," Quentin said. "You want her to be superhuman."

"Listen," Scobie said.

"Love is all there is, it makes the world go round, love and only love, it can't be denied."

"What's it like living at home now?" Matthew asked.

Quentin sighed. "All right. Strange. I can't wait to get to college."

"College isn't so great."

"High school's worse."

"I hate college," Matthew said. "Scobie, how could you have talked me into going?"

"You wanted to go."

"College is boring and being bored makes me sad because it's stupid to be bored. There are millions of things to do that aren't boring."

"Like?"

"I don't know. Traveling."

"You both need to fall in love," Scobie said.

Matthew laughed.

"Seriously. Think about it. If you're in love, you can't get bored. Am I right? And you can't worry about things, you know?"

"Sure, I'd like to fall in love," Matthew said. "Turn the record over."

As Scobie approached the Grundig he thought of the summer nights he and Matthew used to lie in bed listening to friends playing on the street, the voices of their parents rising from the garden on the other side of the house, where they sat drinking coffee, a kerosene lamp picking their faces out of the darkness and throwing the rest of the garden into a flickering confusion of shadows. Scobie and Matthew had slept in other rooms, but this was the one Matthew remembered best. Dylan spoke through the speakers once again.

Scobie lay down on the carpet. "It's their anniversary."

"What're you talking about?"

"Mom and Dad. It's their anniversary, and that's probably a strange time."

"There's also a full moon," Matthew said.

"Just *listen* to that music. We could conquer the world with that music."

"Scobie, you're such a romantic," Matthew said.

"True enough. I believe in the possibility of ecstasy. No doubt about it."

"Your idea of ecstasy is what most people call melancholia," Matthew said.

Quentin was giggling, his hands holding his sides.

"What's so funny? No respect for your elders. That's the trouble with this younger generation."

"Let's go swimming," Matthew said.

"You've lost your mind. It's dark out there."

"Come on." Matthew stood, grabbed Scobie's left hand, Quentin his right, and they pulled him to his feet.

"Middle-class children of the world, unite," Matthew said, running for the door. "You have nothing to lose but your guilt."

Sleep would not come, though Sam imagined islands, the morning light in the room of his childhood, though he recited the names of the girls he had loved in school, the dates of every major nineteenth-century sea battle he could remember. A cool, damp breeze billowed the curtains. He lay on his side of the bed and listened to Laura sleep. She breathed deeply, quietly. The shapes in the room, furniture and shadows, flickered like props in an old movie, burning into the darkness a suggestion of so much more than he could see. Sitting up, he rubbed his eyes. The room burst into flames. Blinking, he restored order. Then he slid from the bed, carefully, trying not to wake Laura. She murmured, rolled over, her hands pressed together beneath her cheek. He groped in the shuttered moonlight for his trousers, pulled them on, picked up his shirt, and tiptoed from the room. If he spoke he would hear nothing. He crossed the hallway. The slow fan whirred overhead. Descending into the dim light of the downstairs hallway, he felt as if he were rehearsing a movement he would later complete, or completing a movement he had already rehearsed. The front door was open and he could see the swimming pool rippling in moonlight, a thousand white birds. Stepping into his study, he turned on the light, poured himself a large Scotch, and sat at his desk, surrounded by wings and struts, propellers and blueprints. He *did* love Laura, at least as much as he wanted to leave her. How happy he was seemed, at this point, a useless question. He was Laura's husband, she was his wife, they were the parents of their children. Both of them believed in what they were doing. Family was a necessary faith. Within families beauties that perished elsewhere thrived and multiplied.

"Hi, Dad."

Sam looked up, surprised. "Hello, Scobie."

"What're you doing?"

"Oh . . ." Sam glanced around at the aeronautical paraphernalia and shrugged. "Nothing, I suppose." He took a long swallow of Scotch and swirled the ice cubes in his glass, staring intently, hoping he might divine, in the motion and clatter, the essence of the day. "What're you doing up this late?"

"Couldn't sleep," Scobie said. "I kept thinking about that crazy scene at the embassy tonight."

"Want a drink?"

"No, thanks."

Again, in Scobie's presence, Sam felt light-headed. "Are you having a good time?"

"This summer, you mean?"

Sam nodded, twirling a propeller blade with his fore-finger.

"Yes," Scobie said. "Though I kind of miss my girlfriend."

"A special girlfriend?"

"I guess so."

"What's her name?"

"Susan Evans. I met her last fall. I was thinking of flying back early so I could spend some time with her before school starts."

"Sounds sensible."

"You'd like her a lot, I think."

"I'm sure I would."

"Dad?"

"Yes?"

"Are you and Mom having a fight?"

"Nothing serious," Sam said.

"Is she having an affair with David Nightingale?"

Sam looked up. "What makes you think that?"

"I don't know." Scobie shrugged. "I can't really imagine it."

"Nor can I. He's not her type."

"Probably not."

"Definitely not." Sam stood, poured himself another drink, and sat back down at the desk. "Anything you want from the States?"

"No, thanks. Will you see Nana and Pa?"

"Sure."

Sam thought of his mother, his father, the bizarre mixture of love and resentment that would greet him when he arrived. His room would be waiting for him, unchanged except for the addition of his sons' summer toys and books. He swallowed his drink, feeling the burn of alcohol and nicotine in his throat. Perhaps I'll write Laura a letter, he thought, picturing his desk by the window at home, the desk from which, years ago, he had written her his first love letter. But what could he say? I'm sorry? He had already done that. He could tell Laura nothing. She probably understood more than he did anyway. He would only be apologizing to himself for his own failure. Knowledge was memory, he had read in college. Perhaps, writing Laura, he could learn what he had forgotten—why he loved her.

"Dad?"

"Yeah?"

"When you were my age, and falling in love with Mom, did you really feel you were falling in love? You know? Or did it just happen?"

"I fell in love, of course. Nothing just happens. You either want it to happen or you don't."

"But what if you don't know what you want?"

"You feel it."

"What if you don't feel it?"

Sam laughed. "Nothing happens."

"But it does. All the time. Day after day."

"I don't know."

"It's a problem." Scobie laughed.

"Scobie, old chum, I hate to hassle you. But tell me again. I'm slow. Why does Matthew want to leave college?" Sam lit a cigarette.

"Dad, are you all right?"

"Fine. Sure you don't want a drink?"

"No, thanks."

They looked at each other.

"Does he think he's responsible for all the terrible things going on?" Sam asked. "Is that it?"

"Partially, yes."

"But he's not. How could he be?"

"Because of who he is."

"Who he is?"

"Your son."

"That's so bad?"

"In a way, yes. But it's not your fault, Dad."

"My *fault?* What are you talking about?"

"Dad, you're you. White, rich—"

"I'm *not* rich."

"Compared to most people, you are. And you went to Harvard, and your wife went to Wellesley. And you work for the government."

"All I want to do is make an honest living and build my goddamn model airplanes," Sam said. "What's wrong with that? You just wait, boyo. It's a bitch."

He stood unsteadily and reached for his glasses. Scobie leaned forward to help.

"I'm all right, I'm all right. Too much to drink, that's all." Sam stared about the room. "You know, I used to think Pa was so strong, but now I look at him nodding in front of that goddamn television and think, He's *weak*. He's nothing. Bones and bones. He has no idea why he's alive. Then I look at myself and think, You're not much better, Sam."

Moving slowly, careful to appear sober, Sam turned off

the light, then stood with Scobie in the dark room, listening to the drone of an airplane passing overhead. Where was it going? Beirut? London? New York? He could imagine the passengers unbuckling their seatbelts, lighting cigarettes, ordering drinks. Soon he would be one of them, flying home.

"I'm your father, Scobie," he said. "That's all."

The World in a Room

YOU bent above me in the dark room, smelling of ink and leather, or tobacco, or whiskey, your beard scratching my cheek as you kissed me and whispered, "You were dreaming."

"Daddy, where are we?"

"Nana's and Pa's."

"Is tomorrow Christmas?"

"That's right."

"Am I sick?"

"I'm afraid so. But don't worry, we're roommates tonight."

I felt the cool place where the sheet tucked around the mattress, listened to the sound of wind in the trees, creaking beams. Sleep lulled and soothed. Headlights slid up one wall, danced across the ceiling, and vanished out the window. You were undressing. I could hear the clink of coins, the jingle of your watchchain, the thud of your shoes. Your bed squeaked beneath your weight. A match flared, too quickly for me to see your face, and then a single red orb, dimming and brightening, floated in the darkness. Your voice exhaled, softly. "Scobie?"

"Yes, sir?"

"What are you thinking about?"

"Nothing."

"Oh, you must be thinking about something." You waited. "Do you know what I'm thinking about?"

"No, sir."

"How beautiful the light will be in this room when we wake tomorrow morning. White light, reflecting off the snow. Would you like me to tell you a story?"

"Yes, sir."

"Well, let's see. Once upon a time there was a little boy who was very sick—"

"That's me."

"And as this little boy was falling asleep in his grand-mother's house, he thought he felt something strange on his shoulders, reached up and touched . . . feathers."

"Feathers?"

"Yes, feathers. Why not?"

"Sam?" It was Mom, moving across the room in her nightgown, leaning over my bed, her hand caressing my forehead. "How is he?"

"Better. Aren't you, Scobie? I'm telling him a story."

"Well, I'll let you get back to it. Good night, darling." She kissed me. "Sweet dreams." Then she walked to your bed, bent down, and kissed you too. "I wish there were enough room for all of us in here. Sleep well."

"Good night, Laura."

She vanished, a pale blur, through the door.

"Now, where was I?" you asked.

"Feathers."

"Oh, yes. Feathers. So the little boy left his bed and stood in the moonlight. There, stretching behind him, were wings. He couldn't believe his eyes, but flexing his muscles, he raised the wings, like a bird. They were real. He walked to the window. Snow glittered outside, sloping toward the sea. He opened the window and stood on the ledge, then pushed away, flapping his wings, and started to fly, awkwardly at first, but more gracefully and self-con-fidently as he rose higher and higher into the cold night air. When he looked down, he saw his grandmother's house, a miniature house, the blue lights on the fir tree in the driveway, the white snow on the lawn, the beach, the sea, the lights in town. Around and around he flew, happier

than he'd ever been, so high in the sky, circling the house, breathing the air . . ."

I struggled, for a moment, to stay with you, but your voice grew fainter, as if you were walking away through a mansion of empty rooms.

The morning after I met you, Laura, I awoke in this room as excited as a child waking on Christmas. The walls slowly brightened, shades of gray lighting my model boats, wood carvings of sailors, the frayed spines of my books. Sitting up in bed, I remembered my drive home alone through the green night, the voices on the radio, my overwhelming joy as I joined the singing and slapped the steering wheel. Of course, I'd known you for years, but at all those birthday parties and picnics, or playing charades and games in the playground, you had simply been one of the little girls hiding in each other's hair. Pipes rattled and coughed. If I blinked, I thought, my room might disappear. I could smell breakfast in the kitchen. I rose and dressed, then walked through Pa's den, the stare of the stuffed green owl, and down the stairs to the kitchen. Mother glanced up from the sink and smiled. "Good morning, Sam." I kissed her on the cheek and poured myself a cup of coffee. Through the window I could see the water changing color as sunlight rushed into the sea. I sipped, both hands clasping the warm cup. The flowered wallpaper absorbed the sun. The kitchen seemed made of light. "Mother?"

"Yes, dear?"

"Do you remember Laura Donahue?"

"Of course. I always liked her mother. So considerate. They moved into town, didn't they?"

"I saw her last night."

"Oh? How nice. Is she well?"

"She's beautiful."

"Beautiful?" Mother straightened above the sink, her startled eyes almost bleached into bone by the sunlight.

Once, you took me down to the sea, set sail that bellied out, taut with wind, held the tiller between your legs, and taught me the balance on plunging, heaving waves that left me walking, to this day, like a sailor. The sunlight was cold, my clothes were wet, the air smelled of canvas and brine and rope, the air echoed the snapping lines, the thumping hull, the swooshing wake. Your legs firmly spread, you were trusting and testing the strength of what you had built, that small blue boat, that dolphin of wood. I could have stretched forward like a figurehead and broken the green waves with my hands. I looked over the terraced walls of water. Land was a memory. Waves slapped the boat. Light fingered down, weaving a world of smaller worlds. High above us, seagulls circled and cried. Waving your hand, you shouted something, your words snatched and tossed by the wind. I crawled toward you over the pitching deck, trying to hear. Your voice rose again, louder, closer. "The light, Scobie!" you shouted, pointing. My hands clawed the deck, I scrabbled like a dog on ice, I saw the distant land, women waving on the lawn. "The light!" you shouted. "The light!"

Parking the old Packard, I climbed some wide steps to a porch, paused, brushed my shoulders, straightened my tie, rubbed my shoes up and down the back of my trousers,

then pressed the brass button at the side of the door. Sudden light pushed back the darkness, the opening door framed me in music, a young woman with red lips smiled and took my hand. Inside, I nodded as if I were listening, my eyes moving from body to body, looking for you. You were sitting on the arm of a couch, a drink in one hand, a cigarette in the other, talking to friends. What was there about walking through someone else's house that made me so happy? Taking a drink from the bar, I wandered toward you, stopping to greet friends I hadn't seen since high school, faces and voices already painfully distant, almost embarrassing. "Good evening, Laura." You looked up, and I knew from the cautious pleasure in your smile that you had seen me arrive and had waited for me to come and speak. "Hello, Sam," you said, introducing me to the people clustered around you, more names and faces I vaguely wished to escape—men dressed, like myself, in dinner jackets, women waving away cigarette smoke and smiling anxiously, as if they'd all forgotten their glasses and couldn't see. I glanced at you. You were glancing away. How many times, I wondered, had we approached each other before, never realizing I'd some day sit down next to you on a couch, a drink balanced on my knee, and try to think of something to say? Are you enjoying college? Do you support Roosevelt? Do you think we'll enter the war? Your silence, your waiting smile, seemed to take my uneasiness into account.

"I remember you used to make beautiful model boats," you said.

"Model boats, yes."

"Have you stopped?"

"No, no, I'm afraid not."

"Good," you said, firmly. "I'm glad."

The music ended in the next room, applause and laughter mingled for a moment with the rattle of ice cubes and glass, the stuttering conversations, and then another song started, a fox trot, and I heard myself asking you to dance. As we walked together across the living room, you took my arm. The weight of your hand burned through my sleeve.

You stood before the wall, your head tilted to one side, as if you were looking at a painting, then took a step forward and gently pressed your palm to the plaster, listening, it seemed, for a heartbeat. The ship's clock was ticking softly on the mantelpiece, the faucet dripped in the kitchen. Standing back, you raised the huge sledgehammer above your head, swinging the weight in circles, leaning with the force, your shoulders hunched, your legs spread, then suddenly stepped forward like a baseball player and brought the hammer smashing into the wall, shattering the plaster, shaking the house. Bricks, battered and chipped, broke away from behind the plaster. White dust billowed, swirling around your feet. Again and again the hammer rose above your head, again and again it tore at the wall, again and again the house shook as if it were about to collapse. Stains of sweat spread across your back and under your arms, sweat beaded your forehead, glistened on your arms. Your shoulders were quivering and your chest heaved so heavily I thought it might burst. Thick slabs of cement and brick fell from the wall and crashed to the floor, exploding in dust. You were swinging the hammer higher and higher, faster and faster, splintering the wall, chips flying and bouncing about the room. Then a hole the size of your head appeared, a patch of blue sky, the willow outside. Taking one last swing, you smashed the wall out into the garden. The room flooded with light, so bright I had to close my eyes. When I looked again, you were stepping through the door of light, laughing.

Mother's birdseed lay on the snow, patterned by the footprints of birds and squirrels. I was sweating inside my overcoat. Touching my fingers to my lips, I turned my face up to the sky. Somewhere, I thought, the flakes must originate, they must have existed in someone else's mind before falling through mine. I breathed deeply, bringing into my lungs, even deeper, into my heart, the bitter tang of the cold air. I caught a snowflake and watched it dissolve in the palm of my hand. You walked toward me, shrugging through the snow, your eyes bright, your cheeks flushed, your hands red and cold as you touched my face. A few birds sang in the trees. As we both sat down I felt within me the pushing body of another life. I saw an evergreen shaped by the snow, a white hunchback veined and boned with branches, heard the thumping rush of sliding snow— an occasional branch shaking free. "Laura, what did you think of me when we were kids?"

"That you were a snob," you said, laughing.

"Me?"

"Yes, you. Never talking, never coming close, so distant."

"I just liked being alone," I said. "That's the only way I could get anything done."

"All I know is, in those days *everyone* thought you were a snob. You still are, in a way. Aloof."

"Laura, why are you saying these things?"

"I'm sorry. I don't know. I guess I wanted to see you moved, upset, anything."

"So I'm phlegmatic as well?"

"You never *talk*."

"I don't think the way you do. Why try to understand what you can't see with your eyes? Maybe I'm stupid."

"No, Sam, no. Anyway, you brought it up. What did you think of me?"

"I can't remember."

"See, I was right. You didn't even notice the rest of us."

"I can't remember, that's all. You were always giggling . . . you had pigtails, and you called everyone Greta Garbo."

"What?"

" 'Good morning, Greta Garbo,' you'd say to me, running down the corridor and giggling."

"Oh, Sam, you're making this up."

"No, I'm not. But you've changed."

"Well, you've changed, too."

Sitting in the snow, your chin resting on your knees, your green eyes reflecting the color of the sea, you were as vivid as childhood yet strangely ethereal, a sound, a touch. Eyes behind your eyes, eyes I couldn't see, looked through the eyes I knew. You smiled, then stood, brushing the snow from your coat, and started walking toward the house, where Pa, angrily scraping ice from the drainpipes, had been watching us from the top of a silver ladder, his jealousy and sadness rising from him like clouds of breath in the cold air.

It was snowing on the statues. The city, the wrinkled surface of roofs shivering beyond the trees, melted the

snow like water, but there in the park the marble faces of
the naked soldiers paled, smoothed as if by fingers, their
dead eyes filling, their empty hands filling. Children in
bright coats chased each other around and around the statues. You held my hand, motionless, aging, your leather
coat and gloves and hat and shoes turning white, your
recent absence, a kind of snow, still heavy on my back. I
felt I was in a bedroom loud with ticking clocks, a bedroom filling with snow. Your seriousness seemed a scolding, a father's finger raised in admonition. Your hand was
powerful, holding mine, as we walked together between the
statues, unspeaking, our feet leaving parallel paths of footprints behind us, small marks of passage as intimate as the
footprints of birds on a beach. Your body's voice spoke
through your hand, I heard the peace you felt moving
shyly, chastely into my blood. The blind eyes of the statues
watched us walk in circles. The children had left. Their
small footprints were filling with snow. The trees looked
like white umbrellas opened above the benches. We traced
the perimeter of the park, looking for something, I couldn't
imagine what, perhaps a way out, the gravel road leading
to the city, perhaps a way in, a way into the center of the
statues, the invisible circle the statues formed, a way into
the snow, a way into each snowflake. I could tell from the
pressure of your hand that you had forgotten I was there.
You were walking alone. An ocean stretched between you
and the white house in which you were born. You were
standing at the edge of the ocean. The falling snow covered you like a robe of white feathers. Your eyes were filling
with snow, your empty hand, stretched to catch a snowflake,
filled with snow.

. . .

I liked your poems very much, but you looked to see if I was lying, anxiously, not wanting to know. "Aren't they silly?"

"Laura, I like them. I like what they're about."

"Who's your favorite writer?"

"C. S. Forester."

"Honestly, Sam, who's your favorite *best* writer?"

"Edgar Rice Burroughs. Who's yours?"

"Fitzgerald. He lived right down the street from you. Did you know that?"

"No."

"Well, it's true. Did you really like my poems?"

"Yes."

I walked to the window and stared at the small cars moving along Park Avenue, the lights coming on in the tall gray buildings, the violet air seething above the city. I could smell your perfume. Your shoulder brushed my arm. Behind you, the apartment waited, the quiet refuge of your mysterious parents, paintings and books crowding the walls, photographs of boxers framed and hanging, a sideboard burdened with bottles, various hallways leading to closed doors. Someone coughed. We both turned. "Oh, Daddy, this is Sam." Your father stepped forward and shook my hand, his coat open and revealing, draped across his expansive belly, the gold chain of his watch. His eyes, scrutinizing me, were yours. "Hello, sir," I said, feeling coarse. His white hair fell back from his forehead in waves, his pink, clean-shaven cheeks glistened, his delicate hands poured drinks expertly as a scientist mixing chemicals. "Do you box?" he asked, passing me a Martini.

"Yes, sir."

"Good, good." He patted me on the shoulder, his eyes

so angry I knew he wished I were dead. Then the anger disappeared and he was smiling kindly, leading me to the chair by the fire. "I used to box myself. Brooklyn. Nineteen twenty. Knocked hell out of Max McGuire. 'Elephant,' they called him. I got him with a one-two left and a right hook he never saw coming. Bam. He collapsed like a bag of beans. Excuse my language. I'm usually very decent, aren't I, Laura? What I'd like to know, Sam, is what you plan to do with yourself."

"I'm trying to paint the light of the desert," you wrote. "The way the light moves across the sand, the black tents, the women with jars on their heads, the camels asleep on their knees. But the light seems to involve a smell, the thinnest fragrance, a memory of night, I suppose, and I can't paint the smell, I mean I can't find a corresponding color. Also, there's a sound the desert has, a kind of airy whisper, for which there is no color—no color I can discover. So, you see, difficulties abound. Your old father loses battles daily. I wake up filled with that light, yet by night I've lost it all, lost all but the desire to feel it again. Last week I bought a nightingale that won't sing. Mornings, you might find me standing before the birdcage, gently coaxing. Last month I built an ornithopter, a blue wooden bird that won't fly. Evenings, I walk along the river, past the dark boats, their sails folded, the creaking ropes, the fires on the beach, the light from windows breaking the small waves into thin rectangles of surf. Women carry pink-and-yellow parasols above their heads, the knotted ivory handles clasped in their hands like flowers. Sometimes after work I fly my Spitfire on the embassy lawn. First I have to turn off all the sprinklers, much to the chagrin of the gardener. Naturally I cut an eccentric figure turning in small circles as my magnificent flying wonder cuts larger and smoother circles through the sky. I'm reminded of childhood, my afternoons at home, Nana and Pa sitting on the porch, talking and watching me run back and forth across the lawn pulling a kite or trying to catch a renegade model airplane. I could hear their voices as one hears voices over a dune. The air was always warm and filled with the smell of burning leaves. How's school, Scobie? Your report card suggests complete ineptness in mathematics. Why? And are you really on the football team? What position? I was, in my time, a loping halfback. My legs were so skinny no one could tackle me. I was a hero, a star. Why won't my ornithopter fly? Have you ever noticed the way light passing through pine trees becomes cold? Sometimes I think the motivating force in my life has been the desire to escape pine trees. On the desert, as on the sea, the light is pure, unfettered by melancholy vegetation. I was promoted this week. Distinguished diplomats shake my hand, grinning like doctors, then wipe their fingers on their velvet lapels. I'm planning another model boat, approximately the size of a pack of cigarettes, which, God willing, should be ready to sail across the mantelpiece in about ten years. You know, when I was your age, this day—my sitting at a desk, in an office —seemed very far away, if not inconceivable. But I knew I'd travel, I knew I'd walk across the map from color to color, continent to continent. I had a vision of a stone wall in sunlight, a perfect patch of beauty. I felt that some day I would turn a corner, in a city far from home, and find that wall. If you asked me today, I'd offer you a drink. We'd sit together on the crumbling veranda, ice tinkling in our glasses, and watch the sunset. Just before dark, I'd turn to you and say, 'It never works out.' And you would stare at me as if I'd just told you I wasn't really your father. Yet I approach corners today as anxiously as twenty years ago. My silence is a way of preparing myself. Did I ever tell you that your great-grandfather was once arrested for threatening to shoot a policeman? Well, he was, rising to his full height on Brooklyn Bridge—which, by the way, he helped build—and raising his small fist (he was a printer—greeting cards, wedding invitations) and promising the puzzled policeman, 'I'm General Richardson and if you lay a hand on me I'll have you shot!' Resisting arrest, threatening an officer. He once said, glaring down the dinner table, deaf and drunk, 'What this goddamn family needs is a goddamn writer.' Painters, he thought, were stupid. But he himself drew the most beautiful portraits of clocks and bridges. Anyway, the one thing I learned playing football is: when in doubt, fall to the ground and writhe dramatically. You'll be carried from the field, honored, without having lost your life to stop some two-hundred-pound full-back, built like a Pontiac and twice as fast, from scoring a touchdown."

The grass wasn't quite green, but the trees were full, and there were groups of softball players out on the fields. Couples sat on blankets reading or talking. The shadows of trees stretched and rippled across the pond and the rowboats. You stepped to the edge of the pond, holding your wide-brimmed hat on your head, and stared at your reflection. I lay back in the sun and closed my eyes. Children swimming laughed and called, "Marco Polo!" Your dress rustled as you settled beside me. I reached up and touched your hair. It was warm from the sun. "The children are beautiful, Sam," you said. "All I can understand is their laughter." I rolled over, leaned on my elbow. Would I ever have children like that? Would they have secret games they played in the park? The rowboats circled the pond. Behind them, through the thick moving foliage of trees, I saw beggars lining the street like a row of dark statues, their hands stretched out before them. A parade passed along the street, soldiers and sailors, flags and bayonets, trumpets, drums, and girls in gold. Old men were fishing in the pond, small boys were sailing their sailboats. I lit a cigarette, enjoying the hot rush of smoke, breathing deeply, exhaling a swirling white plume. The park was a painting I'd somehow entered. Perhaps, if I stood and walked away, I'd leave myself sitting in the painting. Perhaps the painting was already hanging on a wall in a giant's house, a giant's museum, and I was being watched by giant eyes. That's the way I felt. Someone was always watching me, there was always another, invisible presence filling the air between me and the world. I had never doubted that I was painting myself into a landscape, but I'd never even suspected that someone else was painting the landscape. Only faith could keep me sane, faith so fragile that if I reached out, held the corner between my fingers and pulled, the park would peel away to reveal a wall. Sunlight would soothe the faded plaster, the spider's web, the cracked mirror. In the glittering fragments I'd see myself spinning my cigarette over the grass, the question in your eyes as they searched for mine.

.   .   .

Your eyes stared back, then shifted, almost impercep-
tibly, so that you were looking over my shoulder through
the auditorium glass at the green football field and sloping
hillside and thick blue trees. Voices coughed and murmured. I stepped to the edge of the stage. Spectators surrounded you, knees pressed together, hands folded in their
laps. Their faces, in the slanting sunlight, were translucent
as a baby's fingers. I saw a flower, a lace handkerchief, a
beaded purse. I swallowed, clearing my throat, trying not
to embarrass you. Your eyes roved upward, gazing at the
ceiling. I opened my mouth. Words stumbled into the silence. I swallowed, the pages of what I'd written trembling
in my hands, and spoke again. This time white doves flew
from my mouth, flapping above your head, rising to the
ceiling. Startled, you looked at your knees. The sunlight
caught your glasses, two small mirrors in which I saw myself perched on the edge of the stage. My throat dry, my
knees knocking, I continued reading. I stared down at the
paper in my hands, entering the words, reading myself
aloud, forgetting now that I stood before an audience. Ex-
posing myself suddenly seemed so easy. Even my embarrass-
ment pleased me. I was the loud voice at the dinner party,
the drunk at the funeral, the beggar at the opera. Though
I still sensed the listeners around me, I imagined you and
I were alone in the large room and that my words were
echoes, footsteps in an empty church, each word a step in
a complicated, slightly obscene dance. Feet shuffled, skirts
rustled. I clung to my papers. As I neared the end, I al-
lowed myself to look up, once, quickly. You were leaning
out into the aisle, one hand cupped behind your ear, the
other lifting invisible balloons. Louder, you gestured.
Louder. My voice rose into the remaining words, cut short

by rumbling applause. A hundred glass manikins stood and clapped. You stared at the ceiling, watching the birds, blushing.

My hands trembled to your face, pale eyes the green of sea, and gently stroked, as if you were stone, residing warmth, as if I were seeking the memory of sunlight. Then you took my hand and led me through the empty halls, vaulted stone, up the winding tower staircase to your room, where we undressed, our clothes collapsing in circles at our feet. You murmured something I couldn't hear. Your hands were cool and dry, you arched the soft curve of your belly, pliant as a pillow. Buried in your hair, I tasted salt. I held you in my arms and spread your legs with my knees. You smiled and cupped my head in your hands. We loved inexpertly, our bodies fumbling to find each other's needs, not knowing our own, then lay in silence, listening to a distant tennis game. My shirt was draped over the back of a chair. Your breathing beat against my ears. Our tongues touched, ash, said nothing. I kissed you as if I were kissing you goodbye. You responded with an easy softness that surprised me: without opening your eyes, you kissed the air. The sheets were hanging on the floor by your shoes, there was a half-empty glass of water on the bureau. Your eyes followed an invisible bird across the window. You rubbed your toes along your ankle, smiled, the sun in your hair, pulled me onto your belly, wrapping your legs around me, pushing my chest away with clenched fists, grabbing my neck and pulling my lips to your breasts. Then, suddenly, you were still.

"Are you all right?" I asked, touching your shoulder.

"I'm on the ceiling."
"Please, Laura, are you all right?"
"I'm on the ceiling." You laughed. "I'm on the ceiling."

A nurse crossed the tile floor, her thick shoes squeaking, and slammed open the shutters. Light whirled and hummed, an old music I could not place. The nurse returned to the bed, her hands flying wildly as she plumped your pillow, straightened your sheet. "Hello, Dad," I said. Your face was hidden behind the wide nurse who now turned and winked. She passed me, a starched white rustle, and disappeared, closing the door behind her. I looked back at the bed. You were lying with your eyes open, your head resting against the pillows. You hadn't heard me. My legs and arms seemed to swell. I realized I was holding my breath, afraid to move, yet you sensed me, for slowly your head turned, slowly your profile, the small chin and child's nose, collapsed into the shadow of the hand you raised to shield your eyes from the light. I quickly crossed the room to your bed and pressed my face to your cheek. You smiled and pointed to the window. The white room revolved around me, light moving through the hush of the traffic outside. Eyes behind your eyes, eyes I couldn't see, looked through the eyes I knew. What had you seen that could send you so far back into yourself? The door opened and the nurse entered with an enameled tray. Smiling, she placed it on the bedside table and rolled up your sleeve. You didn't move except to raise your arm and grin at me. The nurse took a hypodermic needle from the tray, stuck the needle into a vial, and drew in a full measure of clear liquid. Turning to you, she dabbed your arm with cot-

ton. I could smell the alcohol. The glistening silver needle
punctured your arm and disappeared. The nurse slowly
pressed the liquid into your muscle, then quickly removed
the needle and patted the prick of blood with her cotton.
The needle clattered onto the tray. You rolled down your
sleeve. The nurse left, the door closing behind her as firmly
as an oven. Again, you blushed, relaxing back into your
pillows. You rubbed your cheeks, closed your eyes, lay perfectly still, breathing. I listened, then leaned closer and
smelled your skin. There were two small freckles on your
chin. They were identical, reddish-brown, snuggled in a
crease. Had I forgotten them, or never noticed them?
They're beautiful, I thought—like planets, or flowers. You
slowly breathed, your chest rising and falling beneath the
sheets. "Dad," I whispered. You smiled and your hands
swam toward me in the blue light. I bent and kissed your
smooth, salty knuckles, the mosaic of pale green veins,
grasping your wrist with my lips and gently sucking, tast-
ing you. You were silent, asleep, lost in your skull, lumi-
nous house of hallways and doors. I rose along the muscle
of your arm to your shoulder, your warm neck, your un-
shaven chin. My tongue moistened your dry, parted lips.
"Dad," I whispered again, but you slept, unhearing. I
stood and walked to the window, leaned out into the clear
afternoon. Below, in a garden, two children were squatting
on a gravel pathway, a boy in a sailor suit, a girl in a gray
skirt, playing a game with pebbles and sticks, intent as gods.
Their voices reached me, tossed by the breeze. The windowsill was hot beneath my elbows. I rested my cheeks in my
hands and stared at the children. Then a woman appeared,
scolding, gathered them up, and led them down the pathway to the street.

.   .   .

The door to the doctor's office opened. A young man stepped out. I couldn't remember his name. Passing me, he whispered, "The next letter's Q." I added the new letter to my imaginary chart. Another young man, Sandy, walked into the doctor's office. The door closed, as did my eyes. I projected the chart onto the inside of my forehead. A D T C R Q . . . The rest was a blank. I opened my eyes and waited, trying not to think. Through the single narrow window I saw the tall city buildings, the jagged blue sky. The other young men waiting in line, talking in low voices and shuffling their feet, seemed to be old friends. I thought I recognized a face, a hand, a laugh, a footstep. Some were dressed in suits, others in crumpled khakis and tweed jackets. The door opened and Sandy emerged. He stopped and whispered, "S." I added the new letter, repeating the entire sequence to make sure I knew it all. Bob, or Rob, stepped into the doctor's office. Once again, the door closed. Without my glasses I could barely see it—the door could have been a hole, the beginning of a tunnel. One more person stood between me and the office. Two more letters. I looked at my hands. Grandpa's gold ring flashed on my finger. Someone lit a cigarette and the nurse's voice called, "No smoking, please." On the green wall hung posters of battleships heaving through waves and smiling sailors waving from a beach. Somewhere, a radio was playing Billie Holiday. I started to whistle, remembered where I was, and stopped. Laura, if only you had been there, if only I could have seen you, then I would have had no qualms about lying to the doctor. As it was, guilt was my worst enemy. The door opened. Bob, or Rob, whispered,

"Z." I thanked him and put the new letter in place. One more. If you had been there I could have said, "We'll live in a house by the sea." Or I could have said, "Tonight, after this is over, let's go dancing." You were my passage to another life. I was waiting in line for a ticket. All I had to do was convince the doctor I could see well enough to be an officer. Behind me, the nurse was typing. I stared at the poster of the battleships and tried to believe I was one of the waves, cool and rolling in the sunlight. I knew it so well. I knew everything it felt. It was only a matter of concentration. The door opened. "L." I stepped into the doctor's office. He was a thin, bent man wearing a blue suit twice his size. His hands were white, his fingers dry as he touched my chest, listened to my heart. "Why do you want to be an officer?" he asked.

"So I can afford to get married," I said.

The doctor started to laugh so hard he choked, standing and reeling back toward his desk, dancing in slow motion across the linoleum floor. When he reached the desk, he leaned on the flat varnished surface and closed his eyes like a woman, his thin face flushed and covered with sweat. I stared at him and laughed too, seeing myself blinking blindly, an animal caught in the headlights of a car. "So I can get married," I said again, laughing harder.

You were there but you were not there. Your presence moved like a ghost from room to room. Through the open door I glimpsed your bureau and your bathrobe and the yellow light swirling toward your new shoes on the tile floor. When I entered you had just left. I turned your cufflinks, the loose change, over in my hand. A clock was ticking, loud as my heart. The house was filled with what you had made, paintings and cabinets and tables and boats —perfect objects. The desert surrounded the house, lapping, like the sea, at the white walls, the pink houses, harems, boulevards leading nowhere, the marketplace dark as coffee, the evening voices rising from balconies, prayers from towers that scratched the sky. The light seeped like blood across the carpet. I opened the drawer of your bedside table and found some rubbers. I might have lain down, borrowed your rubber, and filled it with my sperm, but then you would surely have walked into the room, a manila folder under your arm, brown suit crumpled, looking for a wrench, and your face, framed between my arched knees, would have assumed an expression I couldn't imagine. So I locked the bathroom door and masturbated, raised the liquid bones to the light, then dried my hands and returned to the living room. You were probably in your office, smiling good night to your secretary, or covering a legal pad with drawings of airplanes, or walking home past the resentful sentries, or talking, hands in your pockets, to the homesick Ambassador. Now the living room spoke more of your absence than your presence and I began to understand that my desire to be you was greater than my need to be you. If only, I thought, a beautiful woman were to open the door, find me bent above this table arranging words like a man studying a map of his life, or pondering the next move in a game of chess, or solving a jigsaw puzzle. The ticking of the clock grew louder, more insistent, dragging my eyes away from the table, up to the beige couch, the leather armchair, the watercolor of a sailboat at anchor, the squat Grundig, the brass trays. There wasn't a clock in the room. Frightened, I pushed back my chair and started to stand. The door opened, quietly. You walked into the room, a manila folder under your arm, your brown suit crumpled, and looked at me, briefly, smiling, before lowering your face, shyly, and saying, "Scobie, old chum, you'll go blind in this light." You drew the curtains, turned on the lamps. The hidden clock ticked louder and louder. Stooped above the table, one hand resting on my words, the other on the back of my chair, I realized the noise was my heart, beating so loudly I was sure you must hear it. Straightening, I ran my little finger along my eyebrow, and smiled.

"Hopper, Whistler, Vermeer, Bellini, Boudin, Monet." I shrugged, sipping my wine. "Lots of people."

"What do they have in common?" you asked.

"I don't know, Laura."

"They must have something in common. I love Fitzgerald and Twain because they both see something else, another drama more beautiful than our own, playing within our life. What do your painters share?"

I laughed, tipping back in my chair, my hands on the edge of the crisp white tablecloth, and stared at you as if you had just turned a double somersault above the table. The restaurant, buoyant with laughter, made me feel I was falling, not accelerating but floating, like a feather in sunlight. You touched your silverware and stared at the rose in the middle of the table as if it were a photograph. Were you a little girl again, running across the street, the light filling your yellow dress? Was your father sitting in a cool dark room, listening to the radio? Your waiting, puzzled smile reminded me of Mother, the way she'd smile, later that night, when I returned home to this white house by the sea. I smiled and took another quick sip of wine.

"Sam? Are you listening?"

"Yes." Why did you withdraw into a voice I couldn't recognize? "Yes, I'm listening. I don't know what my painters share. The light, maybe. A way of making it comforting. And a love for detail, I suppose. The small things —a dog barking in the background, the dirt on a woman's fingers as she pours the water." But speaking, I found myself fading away, disassociating myself from my words, which I couldn't even hear any more. Instead, I watched your face as you listened. Your head was tilted to one side, a finger pressed against your chin, and your eyes, I realized, weren't listening either, but were watching me, moving from my eyes to my chin to my hands. Neither of us listened, we both let the other look. What I saw was a young woman in blue sitting at a table, her elbows on the white tablecloth, leaning slightly to one side, the shape, the feel of her body suggested by the changing folds in her dress. Her hands looked like the hands of an older woman. They too had a story to tell. She'd grown up thinking all men were fathers. The candlelight created shadows where wrinkles would some day age her face. Then she shivered to life, laughing. I must have said something funny, or you must have seen in my face the expectation of laughter, and, fearing you hadn't heard what I said, laughed. One of the waiters dropped a tray. China and silverware clattered to the floor, startling us both. I felt the corners of my mouth tighten and pinch. Was I making all this up? Or was it really happening? "Laura, will you marry me?"

"Oh, Sam. Of course."

When I arrived this evening, Nana jumped up from the couch, where she had fallen asleep, and thought, for a moment, that I was you. "Sam, I can't believe you're here!" she exclaimed. "It's just like a dream." Her girlish excitement preceded me into your bedroom, then receded, a conversation with the air, as she hurried to the kitchen. Pa ignored me, moving restlessly about the house, his thick hands attacking imaginary tasks. Later, Nana returned to the bedroom, stood in the doorway, plucking her sweater, peering. "You should go to bed, dear."

"Yes."

She moved closer. "Are you writing?"

"Yes."

"What?"

"A letter."

"Oh."

Now it is midnight. Through the window I hear the soothing murmur of the sea, the sifting, chafing pebbles. When you were young, lying in that bed, what did you hear? Nana and Pa talking in the living room? The creaking old house as it sailed into dreams? Sometimes I feel I could spend my life in this room, surrounded by both our childhoods. My Fanner Fifty pistol is here, in the drawer that always sticks. Your model airplanes, wood carvings of sailors, and Uncle Wiggily books are here, crowding the bookshelves. The room smells of rain and fresh sheets, dew and cedar. The lamp casts a perfect oval upon the desk, and within the oval is this paper, the shadow of my hand moving from margin to margin. I tell myself I'm translating the silences in your head, but I could also be imagining your entire existence. Only you might be able to explain the difference, and your thoughts remain locked in secrecy. I must guess at them, the way, as a child, in this same room, I once guessed at the contents of a Christmas present. Do you remember? I was sick, and you carried the present in from the living room. It was an Indian war bonnet. I never could have guessed. I couldn't even see your face. Tonight I'm back where I began, in your room, staring through the window at the sound of moths pinging against the screen. Beyond the black shapes of the rose bushes I can see the headlights of a car rounding the corner at the foot of the hill, flooding the driveway, dimming into darkness. The motor ticks under the hood. Then the car door opens and the light blinks on inside, illuminating the face of a young man, dark-haired, bearded, wearing horn-rimmed glasses and a dinner jacket. The door slams shut, footsteps crunch across the gravel, a key scrapes at the front door of the house, and the music of crickets reaches a crescendo and falls silent before I realize it's you, feeling, for the first time in your life, the possibility of my existence. You walk into this room, light a cigarette, inhale deeply, balance the cigarette on the edge of the ashtray, exhale, push up your glasses, and lift a copper bird from the desk. Finely textured wings, veined and thin as tissue paper, curl in the light, reflecting gold circles. The bird, beak open, tries to breathe the light, or sing into the light, a stillness poised in silence. Resting the bird on the desk, you walk to the window, draw the curtains, whistling Gershwin as you move around the room, pausing to wind the ship's clock, stare at the rigging on the miniature frigate, examine the drying waves of the seascape propped on an easel in the corner. Then you undress, slip between the sheets, turn off the light, smoke a last cigarette, toss in bed, settle, sleep, and dream of the woman who is to become my mother. In your dream she's holding me up to the light. I'm a waving, squirming baby, and from that great height in her arms I can hear you laughing.

Travel Stories

For a moment, after delivery, Susan had felt herself sliding down a long tunnel of darkness, Dr. Crawford's voice still singing, "Push, *push.*" When she awoke, Scobie was there, at the foot of her bed, breathing. And in his arms he held their child. "Sammy," he cooed. "Sammy, my boy." She had made him a father—that was her first thought. Remembering, she wondered why. Loving Scobie was too much her life, she knew it would hurt her some day.

"Swish!" he cried, feigning a jump shot as he hurried into the living room.

"Have fun," she said.

"Thanks." He kissed her. "I'll be back in a couple of hours."

"Don't kill yourself."

"I won't."

The screen door slammed behind him. She watched him cross their short lawn. Shadows followed. Butterflies? Robins? And was that a crow, perched on the telephone wire? Solemn Sammy, almost three now, sat with Tommy Delano behind their lemonade stand, Mrs. Delano's card-table, and waited for customers. Scobie stopped and bought a cup. They stared in amazement as he finished it in one swallow. Then he waved goodbye and disappeared down Johnson Street, too thin, his hair long, wearing jeans yet carrying himself with a considered air. My fragile, stubborn husband. She looked at her garden, careful rows of tomatoes and zucchini, peas and squash, lettuce and spinach.

Just to the left, her pear tree spun a web of light across the grass. With her help it had survived the winter, something it was not supposed to do, something her friends had said was impossible in Iowa. Would it survive another? Yes, she thought. Or we'll move to California. Scobie could teach at Berkeley, or Stanford, or UCLA. She used to believe, as a child, that when she closed her eyes at night people small as her dolls would slip from the dark hedges and dance in circles around the trees outside.

"Mommy! Mommy!" Sammy nearly pulled the screen door off its hinges as he charged into the living room.

"Sammy, what's wrong?"

He tugged her back to the door. "Look!"

A parade was passing along Johnson Street, about twenty beautiful women wearing white wedding dresses and carrying signs. I AM WHO I AM, one sign said. LET ME BE, another read. Taking Sammy's hand, Susan stepped out onto the front stoop. Neighbors clustered at their doors and smiled curiously. The women danced, taking small dainty steps through the stillness. A few carried umbrellas, also white, open against the heat. One of them crossed the lawn to the stoop and offered Sammy a rose, the wilting yellow flower pinched between square dirty fingers, a man's fingers, Susan realized, looking closer and seeing the bristles of a beard behind the rouge. She quickly pulled Sammy away, holding him.

"Mommy, what's wrong?"

"Nothing, sweetheart."

"I wanna see!"

"Of course." She kissed the top of his head and let him go. "I'm sorry."

She stood still for a moment, trying to steady her breathing. Sammy obviously had no idea that the beautiful women were men. He just liked the excitement. She could see him back behind the lemonade stand with Tommy. The parade had turned the corner and vanished. Some vision, she thought, crossing the living room and walking into the kitchen. Here the sunlight was brilliant, shining directly into the room, and as she moved between the sink and the shelves, stacking clean plates and glasses, she felt she lived in a treehouse. She turned on the radio. "Terrorists holding sixty hostages today agreed . . ." Mahler replaced the news. She wiped the counter and table with a sponge, then swept the floor. Sammy should be taking his nap now. But if she let him stay up he would fall asleep earlier tonight. She bent down into the cool breeze of the refrigerator, throwing away old vegetables, a soggy salad, a yogurt gone bad. What could you say to a man who wanted to be a woman? Or a woman who wanted to be a man? What could you say to someone who wanted to change herself that much? She returned to the sink and washed her hands, looking through the window at a red toy truck on its side in the grass.

The black guy covered Scobie closely as they nudged each other back and forth beneath the boards, shifting for position, absolutely silent, almost embracing. He out-weighed Scobie by twenty pounds. His thick squat legs moved with the tireless precision of someone still in perfect shape. Scobie could taste every cigarette he had ever smoked, he could hear the rush of blood in his ears, his legs wobbled weakly. But he continued to run, fake, maneuver for rebounds, wondering if his heart would explode or splinter or simply stop. Somehow he reached the other end of the court in time to help Groggy pick and roll. The ball swished through the net. Steve tapped Scobie on the shoulder. "Nice game." Slowly Scobie walked into the hallway, through the swinging doors to the locker room. This smell, a smell of brutality, had once terrified him. Now it calmed, familiar and restful. He opened his locker and stripped, then hurried to soak beneath the hot shower, his face lifted into the force of the steaming water, his muscles easing luxuriously. The echoing cavern of white tiles seemed some foggy passageway to another life. All the men knew it, they shared the presentiment. Naked as victims, they joked, laughed, bellowed Top Ten hits, playfully snapped towels, uneasiness behind every move. Scobie returned to his locker through a long aisle of green metal doors stretching toward a shaft of light leaning against the ribbed radiator. The voices in the shower were distant now. He was already sweating, the subterranean humidity much worse than anything outside. A few pale naked figures drifted past. Slamming his locker door closed, spinning the dial of the combination padlock, he moved to the wall of sinks and mirrors, incongruously clothed, suddenly claustrophobic as he hurried through the swinging doors and up two levels of concrete steps to the main hallway. It was empty, the lights off, a perspective of narrowing walls reaching down to the doors, each wall covered with framed photographs of football players and swimmers and track stars whose dim smiles and shy eyes peered at him curiously as he passed between them, trying not to look back. He pushed open the heavy door and stepped outside, overwhelmed by the hot air. Summer students sat on the grass waiting for the bus. Others hurried toward town, swinging bookbags. "Reading fiction makes certain subtle demands of the senses, demands difficult to understand let alone meet"—so he had started his class this summer. "The *attraction* is the attraction of any experience: expanding your consciousness. The *danger* is what can happen along the way." God, he bored himself sometimes. His students listened with nodding blond faces, scrupulously taking notes, dreaming of other journeys, the real life they somehow managed to take seriously. Professor Richardson indeed. What a joke. The birds were singing. Rather raucously, he thought, and laughed. Sitting down on the grassy ridge overlooking the river, he lay back with his hands behind his head and stared at the sky, so clear of clouds it looked painted, a perfect unmottled blue, the inside of a beautiful bowl. He could have reached up and pinned a substantial cumulus, or a wispy cirrus, to the expressionless heavens. Megalomaniac. He closed his eyes. Imagine nothing. Smell and hear and touch what's there. Voices carried clearly but incoherently from the riverbank—more students, playing guitars and throwing frisbees. Sometimes he thought desire was only the perfect re-creation of an original sadness. Loving Susan, he could feel all the other men falling backward, all the other women waiting for definition, all the years spent by everybody looking for everybody.

"Mommy, where's Daddy?"

"Playing basketball."

"Why?"

"Sammy, please don't ask so many questions. I'm trying to work. Have you seen the bucket?"

"When's he coming home?"

"Soon." She searched among the bottles and paper bags under the sink. "Would you please go into the living room?"

"Why?"

"Sammy."

He stared at her helplessly from the middle of the kitchen floor, turned and walked away, sneakers squeaking on the linoleum, shoulders stooped, head hanging.

"Sammy, what're you doing?"

"Nothing."

"Nothing what?" She peered around the corner. He was sitting cross-legged by the couch, his back to her. "Come on, let's work in the garden."

He reluctantly joined her, already anxious to grow up, escape. If only you knew, she thought, watching his green eyes, speckled gold out here in the sunlight. She handed him a spade. "Can you dig a little tunnel for me? Right along the edge. Like this. It's for the water."

He studiously set to work, the spade unwieldy in his small hands. She pulled weeds. The soil was dark and damp, the best outside someplace in Russia. The Ukraine, maybe. Sunlight lay on the grass like a panting dog. A few cars passed, sounding imperative, going somewhere. A bicycle clattered over the curb. She stopped working and stared intently at the Delanos' cluttered backyard, the corner grocery store with its bright red Coke machine by the door, the sandstone Catholic church across the street. Downtown in the bars, she knew, men and women her age were already drinking beer and watching baseball on television as they collapsed drunkenly into fitful camaraderie, pounding each other's backs and rivaling to pay for rounds. It'll hit a hundred tomorrow, she thought, bending back to work, trying to ignore the thickness of the air. Surrounding downtown were these frame houses, porch swings, cobbled alleys, these streets quiet as Sunday. She had taught third grade until Sammy was born, the sinking fear she had felt as a child in school returning every time she passed through that heavy green door and heard her footsteps tap-tap-tapping along the hallway, the children's voices squealing and shrieking no matter what they said because they assumed no one was listening. Past the water cooler she had hurried, past the bulletin boards and the teachers' room, which she feared even more than her classroom, it was more knowingly in despair. Even remembering, it made her sick. Motherhood had come as something of a relief. Last night she had asked Scobie if he thought she was stupid. Now why did I do that? It's just the kind of question he hates. "Sammy, be careful, don't cut those roots. See?"

"Mommy, when's Dad coming home?"

"Soon. You can stop now, if you want. Why don't you go play in your sandbox?"

"Okay." He trudged off. Poor kid. She was always suggesting things for him to do. She stood and squinted dizzily into the sun. There was Mrs. Delano, Tommy's grandmother, waving from the porch next door. "Hello," she called, guiding herself carefully down the steps and approaching Susan across the driveway that separated the two houses. "How's your garden coming along?"

"Fine, Mrs. Delano." Susan waited for her to arrive before asking, "And how are you today?"

"Getting older, I believe." Mrs. Delano stopped a few feet away, catching her breath. "What a lovely garden."

"Thank you."

"My son doesn't want a garden. Can you imagine?" She shook her head sadly. "Am I bothering you?"

"Not at all."

"I know I'm a bit talky. How's Sammy?"

"Just fine."

"He and Tommy are quite close now, aren't they? Though, between you and me, I think your son is more *intelligent*." She whispered the last word, glancing guiltily over her shoulder toward her house. "That woman," she said, looking back at Susan. "Bad blood. How old are you, dear, if I may ask?"

"Twenty-nine."

"When I was twenty-nine I went to Chicago." She appraised her thick, short fingers. "Have you ever been to Chicago?"

"Once. I didn't like it much. I don't like cities."

"Awful places. Cliff dwellers. Where's your husband?"

"Working."

"Such a nice young man." She smiled demurely. "I watch him."

"Oh?"

"From my window. I saw him bury a bird yesterday."

Susan shuddered, as if Mrs. Delano were telling her something she was not supposed to know. "A bird?"

"Yes. A small bird, maybe a robin. My eyes don't work well any more, even with my glasses. I need a new prescription. Do you wear glasses?"

"To read."

"So unattractive, I think, don't you?" She was young again, trading beauty tips. "My father went to the grave never needing glasses. My mother too. Stone deaf, though. Both of them."

There was a general shifting of weight beneath Mrs. Delano's baggy calico dress. She folded her arms and surveyed the garden with a pleased eye, her white hair as downy as Sammy's. "I talk too much." She slowly focused on Susan. "No point in that, is there? You go on and start dinner. I've bothered you enough for one day."

Susan said nothing, hating herself. Mrs. Delano smiled, straightened her hair, tentatively waved. "Goodbye."

Her stolid figure moved toward the shadows. She was knee-deep in death, bored by what she had made—her son, his family—and frightened because she had made nothing else.

"Goodbye," Susan called, dread drying her mouth. "See you tomorrow."

From his office window Scobie watched a woman cross the street below, squint uncertainly, her hand shading her eyes, then turn and walk away, mingling with a crowd of students moving toward the Union. The window was hermetically sealed. He stared at the place on the curb where she had stood, the easeful slope of green grass. Behind him, his small desk lamp could only pick a pool of funneled motes from the darkness. Air-conditioning circulated, stale, acrid. Whom had the architects imagined working here? Robots? Catatonics? He reached over and opened his desk drawer, rifling some two-year-old parking tickets, small sugar bags, a wooden coffee stirrer, irritated at himself for sinking back into his old yearnings, this hopeless, childish expectation that made him long for his life with Susan before Sammy was born, the clear evening shadows that used to stretch across the balcony of their rented room on Crete. He peered back through the window at the clock on the capital tower. A few gleaming cars, great silver fish, caught the light in bursts, finned sluggishly away. He scooped up the books he had come to get and walked to the elevator, descended, and left through the open lobby of brick walls and glass doors. The moist air was almost a relief, proof he lived and breathed. He stood on the hot soft tar waiting for his body to catch up with his head. Then he passed under the concrete railroad bridge —a blur of moss and graffiti, short echo, darkness—and started the slow climb past the library. The wide blue sky stood brilliant, electric, behind the darkening buildings. Starlings darted like bats in the shrinking light. The light, almost liquid, reminded him of something else. What? He turned, startled by a burst of rock-and-roll, early evening excess obscure in the receding blackness of Peter's Tavern —a jukebox, dull purple, gleaming. Suddenly churchbells rang, soft and steady in the stillness. Scobie stopped and blessed the Catholics. They rang their bells with papal regularity, even here, in the heart of nowhere. Mothers called their children in to dinner. Screen doors slammed, springs pinging. A girl in a yellow dress skipped rope in front of the hospital, counting monotonously, dreamily. He stepped across the stretch of grass and into the kitchen. Susan was at the sink, slicing onions. He kissed the back of her neck. She turned and smiled and touched his cheek, her fingers wet. Her eyes went on forever. He held her tight, frightened, as always, by the smallness of her bones. "The good guys won."

"Congratulations."

The kitchen window was open. A warm sweet breeze rustled some papers on the table. He smelled lilac, cut grass, smoking hamburgers. "Let's cook out tonight."

"Wonderful! Sammy would love that."

"Where is he?"

"In his sandbox. Talking to himself." She grinned, crying
—the onions.

"I'll start the charcoal," he said, touched by her false
tears.

He opened the screen door and paused on the concrete
step, looking over the grass—he would have to mow it
tomorrow—at the thick wall of bushes and drooping willows that shadowed the Delanos' yard. Three white
wooden chairs and a white table turned pale purple in the
changing light. He inhaled deeply, noisily, closing his eyes
and trying to relax his arms, his shoulders, his tight aching
neck. When he opened his eyes, the lawn, the bushes and
trees, the chairs and table all seemed to have just stopped
laughing. He walked around the corner of the house.
Sammy sat in the middle of his sandbox moving toy trucks
through a wilderness of collapsing mountains.

"Hello, Sammy," Scobie said, so quietly he could barely
hear himself. "Sammy?"

Those pink fingers, the delicate moons, waved in delight above the cooling sand. "Daddy!" A brief, imaginary em-
brace: "Daddy!" Or was he merely including Scobie in his
secret world, the cause of all that pensive seriousness, so in-
tense for a child so young? Scobie crossed to the red
sandbox, bent down. "How're things?"

Sammy looked into the sand, puzzled, his eyes partially
Susan's, partially Scobie's father's, partially no one's.
"Daddy?"

"Yes."

"Tommy's father makes trucks."

"I know." Scobie laughed.

Through the light caught by the leaves he finally saw
what the afternoon had felt like all along, another, similar

afternoon when he had stopped in Great Neck and found Fitzgerald's house. White stucco walls, Normandy tower, lawns, swimming pool, even a blinking green light on the bay—it was exactly as described in *The Great Gatsby,* so much so that he had expected to see Gatsby himself come strolling out onto the terrace and wave to him across the vibrating lawn. What was this craving for vividness, the liquid bliss of total immersion? Scobie ran his hands through the sand. It was still warm from the sun. An airplane flew overhead as the perfect balance between day and night passed. The whole world quivered, threatening to vanish, but he stared and forced the sandbox to remain on the lawn, he forced the lawn to meet the uneven blues of the trees. "Come on, Sammy. Let's go help your mother get dinner ready."

Their mouths moving slowly and silently, Scobie and Sammy looked like two men discussing the weather, the war, something serious. Sammy, trying to imitate his father, leaned with his weight on one leg, his hip slightly cocked, his hands in his pockets. Susan quickly concentrated on the salad, humming an old hymn as she moved about the kitchen. She carried the salad out to the wooden table in the backyard.

"Hi, Mommy," Sammy greeted her. "Look what we're doing."

"What's that?" She unwrapped the paper plates, distributed the paper napkins.

"Trying not to burn supper is what we're doing," Scobie said, banging at the grill.

"How much longer?" she asked, heading back toward the screen door.

"Five minutes."

The house was already dark. She turned on a few lights as she made her way to the bedroom and changed, remembering nights like this when her father, splendid in his white tuxedo, would prance about the kitchen playing Louis Armstrong on his trumpet. Then off he would go to a club, where his band entertained strangers until one in the morning. She stared at herself in the mirror, brushing her hair. Susan, where have you gone? Away. College. Europe. Marriage. Motherhood. She looked deeper into her own eyes and saw a young girl sitting on a bed, rain sliding down the windowpanes behind her. Too much dope. She resumed brushing. Susan, where have you gone? Dancing, crazy, to the movies, nowhere, *I don't know*. It was an impossible question, a voice speaking from her worst fears, and she resolutely ignored it, dropping her brush onto the bureau, next to Scobie's watch, and leaving the bedroom. Yet the words, like a jingle, ran through her head, nightmarishly persistent. She pushed open the screen door and stepped out onto the grass. Scobie was busy seasoning the hamburgers. Sammy pushed toy trucks toward an inevitable and colossal collision.

"Mommy, I'm *hungry*."

"Dinner's ready," Scobie called. "Come and get it."

They carried their paper plates to the grill, then sat together at the wooden table, passing potato chips and ketchup while around them the shadows lengthened and the birds gradually grew quiet.

"Hi," Scobie said, grinning at her.

"Hi."

"What do you think?"

"About what?"

"This." He laughed. "Our future. It's here."

"I think it's fine," she said.

"Me, too."

"But weird."

He nodded, his eyes moving to the closing circle of darkness. Susan leaned back and stared at the pink and purple sky. Soon it would be drained black. The air's so clean out here, she thought, breathing deeply. Yet she missed the ocean, the strong salt breeze rolling in with the waves, the fog, the dampness, the sweet brackish stink of low tide, those long slow days on the beach. At night the lights exploded along the old boardwalk, the Casino burned at the edge of the sea, thousands of kids strolled back and forth, eating cotton candy, smoking joints, trading albums on the steps of the bandstand where her father once played afternoon concerts. She had been one of those kids, one of too many. Where she came from, fathers worked in factories or for the government, mothers raised children, and everyone went to church on Sunday. She thought of her mother, smiling, rueful and scrutinizing as she turned from the kitchen sink, the slender white lighthouse balanced in the window behind her, an obsolete warning rising from a cluster of rocks and seaweed half a mile offshore.

"Daddy, how come I don't have a brother?" Sammy asked.

Susan jumped. "What?"

"Tommy has a brother."

"Virgil Smith has a sister," Scobie said, peering into his salad.

"How come I don't have a sister?"

"Most kids get jealous when they have a brother or sister," Susan said.

Sammy shrugged his shoulders. "How come we're not going anywhere this summer? Tommy's going to Florida."

She reached across the table and wiped his mouth with her napkin.

"We can't afford to go anywhere," Scobie said. "We don't have enough money. But maybe next summer. How'd you like to go to New Hampshire? See your grandparents?"

"Oh, boy."

"Really?" Susan asked.

"Sure. Why not? If we've got the bread."

"That would be lovely," she said. "I miss them."

"I know you do."

Sammy had pulled his hamburger from the bun and was now holding it above him and nibbling at the edges.

"Eat that thing right or don't eat it at all," Scobie scolded.

"Hey, folks."

It was Joey, crossing the grass with Clara, Susan's oldest friend in Iowa City and an intern at the nearby hospital. They had met at a party, Susan immediately liking Clara's wide, welcoming face and big-boned softness, the enthusiasm in her gray eyes. Joey was as angular as she was curved, as dark as she was fair, a silent nodding elf with a habit of smiling before he asked you a question, pleased by its appropriateness, the possibilities of the answer. He played drums for a local band. Clara's red hair bounced at her shoulders and when she smiled she positively beamed. "Happy Fourth of July."

"You, too."

"So what's happening?" Joey grinned, a wrinkle of his rabbinical beard.

"Not much," Scobie said. "Just a nice suburban scene here. Want a beer?"

"Sure. Hey, Sammy." Joey touched Sammy's dirty cheek. "When're you going to learn how to play the drums?"

Sammy thought. "Soon."

．　．　．

Susan loved parties, the quick rush of excitement she felt when friends or strangers arrived at the door or when she first walked into someone else's room and realized that within the next few hours anything at all could happen. Along with sex, a party was the only human enterprise organized around the simple principle of pleasure. Of course, sex had not always been that way. Her parents thought it was a command to have children, a necessary and rather embarrassing technicality. At least, that was what they seemed to believe. Who could tell? Not me, she thought. Scobie made love with the sad precision and distant thoughtfulness of a priest administering last rites. Afterward, they curled together like children, their small protected space something to defend from the outside world, the attacking forces—time and loss, disbelief, fear, the sure knowledge that pleasure seeks oblivion, annihilation, escape. Susan moved into the kitchen, compulsively wrapping vegetables in cellophane and pushing them into the refrigerator. Clara kept her company, leaning against the counter, the screen door behind her neatly dividing the summer night into small square mosaics. Susan could hear Sammy laughing happily as he sat on Scobie's chest on the living room floor, miming aggression while Scobie mimed horror, neither of them speaking, only the Beatles' ironic, nervous music accompanying their struggle.

"Sammy, bedtime!" she called.

"Aw, Mommy," he groaned, breaking the spell. "Do I have to?"

"Authority speaks." Scobie laughed.

"Daddy, do I have to?"

"Yes, you do. I'll take you up. Tell you a story. Okay?"

"Yes, sir."

"So let's go." Scobie stood. "Say good night."

Sammy, slipping his hand from Scobie's, ran to Susan. Did he love her more? Scobie remembered his own father's threatening power, that silent shape refusing softness. Susan's plants broke the dim light into crazy shadows. Scobie stared at the ghostly green aquarium, the flicking, darting fish, the mother-of-pearl cigarette box he had inherited from his grandmother, his wall of books. Two black speakers, large as coffins, stood upright in the corners.

"Good night," Sammy said to Joey, returning and taking Scobie's hand again. They climbed the stairs together, the music muffling behind them. Susan looked up as Joey hesitated in the kitchen doorway. "Hi. We're just talking."

He entered warily. "Any more beer?"

"Of course. I'm sorry. In the fridge."

He leaned down into the green light. "So what's up?" he asked, straightening and pulling the beer top.

"Nothing," Susan said. "We were just wondering what it would be like to all sleep together."

"Are you serious?"

Even before they started laughing Susan wondered what it *would* be like. Scobie would never do it, though. He was too conservative. She could almost hear him: *Fathers don't do that sort of thing.* He and Sammy would often sit up there for hours, Sammy listening transfixed as Scobie told him about trees that talked and oceans that thought, her own voice reaching them as a reassuring murmur. "Would you be scared, Joey?" she asked.

"Disgusted."

"Why?"

"All that flesh."

Following him back into the living room, Susan sat on the floor, resting on one of the large bright pillows, and rolled a joint. Scobie would not smoke any more. She wondered what reveries did to a surreal imagination, then wondered what they had already done to hers. Clara held her chin high, a touch of stubbornness in the stance. Susan stared at the shape of her loose breasts beneath her dress, her thin hands, smoothing her lap. Clara took the joint and puffed delicately, her little finger cocked, as if the joint were a cup of tea, eyes squinting in concentration. Scobie returned, smiled at them, and made himself a Scotch. For a few seconds Susan resented his overview.

"Sammy okay?" she asked.

"Oh, yeah, he's fine." Scobie shook his head, refusing the joint, as he stretched out beside her. "You know, he thinks I make all those stories up. He thinks all the myths I tell him are mine."

Susan laughed, clapping her hands, that girlish, delighted gesture she knew he loved.

Scobie grinned at the ceiling. "He probably thinks I'm a lunatic and just listens to humor me."

"Scobie, I have a big favor to ask you," Joey said.

"Change the record."

"Thank you."

Clara nodded vigorously, red curls dancing around her temples, the imaginary teacup still balanced in her hand. Scobie crawled to the stereo. "I first saw the Beatles in nineteen sixty-four," he said. "Twelve years ago. Incredible, huh? Any requests?"

"Something cheerful."

"Something bouncy."

"Aretha Franklin?"

"Let's dance," Susan said, clapping her hands again.

"Dancing it is." Scobie stood, pulled her to her feet, and led her around the room in an exaggerated waltz to the pure round notes of "Dr. Feelgood." Energy's the rush that comes with rock-and-roll, everything private made public, celebrated. He swirled Susan under his arm, dancing awkwardly, self-consciously, his eyes on Clara. He trusts me, Susan thought. But I can't trust him, not completely, there's the difference. Then she wondered if she also loved him more, if her lack of trust were the result of that difference. Scobie, needing her less, trusted her more? Did that make sense? One thought and Scobie lost the rhythm. He watched Susan to catch it again. Slowly he was back in the music. Clara saw him looking and smiled. He smiled too, more with his eyes than his mouth, a secret message sent over Susan's shoulder. Or was Susan imagining things? Was he just being friendly? She glanced around the room. The fish in the aquarium seemed to swim to the music. Even their air bubbles were synchronized. Everything works that way, if you can see what's happening. She looked at Scobie. We're a beautiful couple, she thought. Friends said it, parents said it, employers said it, Susan had even heard strangers saying it: "What a beautiful couple." Beautiful couples don't have problems. Why had she ever believed that? Neither of them was really beautiful, she knew. They were pretty and graceful. They seemed to know what they were doing. She almost laughed, watching him now, gangly as a tourist trying to belly dance, his serious face concentrating on the impossible task of gyrating elegantly. "Won't the music wake Sammy?"

Scobie turned it down. "I don't think so."

"It might," she said. "Maybe we should wait a while."

The song ended and they were left staring at each other in silence, kids again at their first dance, wondering what to say, how to stand. They all sat down.

"We're irresponsible parents," Susan said.

"No, we're not," Scobie said. "Children like to hear music. I can remember lying in bed and hearing my parents having parties. They played Frank Sinatra, that's the only difference."

"A little less loudly," she said.

"Maybe. I felt very secure hearing all that noise. And the laughter. They sounded happy."

Susan was watching him the way his mother had once watched him try to flirt. There's no escape from familiarity. He had to live with it, as he lived with bad weather, his own depression, guilt, the power of stupid and spiteful people. Only when love is a duty are we eternally secure against despair. He let himself really look at Clara for the first time since they met, though he remembered that night, her slow movement toward him through the laughing couples, a smile ready on her face, dressed in jeans and a red silk shirt open low enough to expose the smooth white beginnings of her breasts, so much larger than Susan's, swaying as she leaned forward to tap her cigarette ash into an empty paper cup. She was very beautiful, a northern star, pale as breath on a cold window. He had always imagined her life as a series of outings. To football games, snug in plaid blankets. To picnics and parties. To the coast in a crowded station wagon.

"Scobie?" She was offering him the joint.

He shook his head.

"How come you don't smoke?" she asked.

"I lose control."

"Of what?"

"Whatever it is that convinces me I'm only one person."

Laughing as she took the joint, Susan let her fingers brush Clara's, then quickly looked toward Joey, as if she were interested in what he was saying, or the smile on his face, that dreamy, tranquil expression he assumed when stoned or happy. Even my fantasies are clichés, Scobie thought, changing the record again. Two women tongue to tongue, nipple to nipple. He had once dreamed of singing with a rock band, swaying obliviously as his own voice boomed back at him, finally finding a beat indistinguishable from the heart's. That would be happiness. Smoking dope and listening to music always reminded Susan of college, those four fast years when she had almost escaped her entire childhood. Now that freedom seemed as ephemeral as any other. Nothing's in control because it all comes rushing at you a million miles a minute, nameless, contorted, laughing like God: What do *you* know, Miss La-De-Da? Not much, she thought.

"Are you going to teach again?" Clara was asking.

"Soon as Sammy gets a little older."

"What if you have another kid?" Joey asked.

"We'll deal with that when and if it happens." Scobie solicitously drew her closer. He smelled of sweat, tobacco, an old smell she loved, man-smell, father-smell.

"I'm not sure I want to have another kid," she said.

"I *know* we can't afford it," Scobie said. "But it'd be a shame for Sammy not to have a brother or sister, don't you think?"

"Yes," she admitted.

"He'd be very lonely. It's a trap," he continued, explaining to Clara. "You have one kid, then you feel morally obliged to have another to keep the first one company, and the next thing you know you're fulfilling all your statistical expectations. Gotcha."

The truth being, of course, that he wanted to have another child, but thought Susan wanted to be able to walk into a room and tell people she was more than a mother. "I don't resent being a mother. There'd be no point to that."

"It doesn't really make much sense, though," he said. "Why put kids through all the shit you've just been through? They're not going to help you run the farm, or maintain your membership in the House of Lords. Right? If you have children, you've got to admit you're having them for your own pleasure. There's no other reason any more."

"Propagating the species."

"Propagating the *class,* you mean. Or the race. What's the point?"

"So why did you have Sammy?" Clara asked.

"I'm sentimental."

Bliss, that's what he wants, and that's why he loves children, they seem so much closer to the source. Susan had always found it strange that someone who loved language so much should consider silence truth. She could never be sure what he was feeling.

"My father wanted me to marry and settle down," Clara said. "The whole thing."

"And now you're a hot-shot doctor. I like that."

This time Susan was sure he exchanged a look with Clara, a quick, sheepish grin.

"It'll be dark in a few minutes," he said. "We should go out."

"I can't move," Joey said.

"Pothead."

"Moralist." Joey rolled over and looked at Scobie.

"Come on," Susan said. "Let's go out."

They stood and went out together to the backyard, where they lay on their backs, staring at the sky and talking while beyond the trees a fierce red streak grew thinner and slowly sputtered away, leaving behind the sudden night. Then a Roman candle shot hissing high above them and exploded, showering down a soft umbrella of smaller stars. Susan flinched when the next explosion hit the sky. It was spectacular, terrifying. She could feel Scobie's arm touching her elbow.

"Napalm," he said.

"Oh, Scobie. Don't be disgusting."

"Sorry. Just free-associating."

"Do you think it'll wake Sammy?"

"It might," he said. "Jesus, can you imagine? He'd probably think it was World War Three."

"Scobie, he doesn't even know what war is."

"You know what I mean. The end of the world. Cataclysm. Holocaust. Apocalypse. I'd better go check."

He rose and disappeared into the house. Joey lit another joint and passed it around. Susan took it all the way in this time, holding her breath until it hurt. The explosions vibrated, painfully explicit.

"Clara, do you ever wish you had kids?" She giggled. "Tell me the grass is always greener."

"I envy you sometimes, sure."

"We ought to start a mutual admiration society. You've got freedom. You're making something of yourself."

"You sound like my father," Joey said. "Clara's just trying to get along, like everyone else."

"Clara's a woman who hasn't let her entire life be determined by what a woman's expected to be," Susan said. "In case you hadn't noticed."

"I'd noticed."

"I don't particularly like being a doctor," Clara said. "Not all the time."

"Excuse me while I slit my wrists."

"You don't understand, Joey," Susan said. "We're having a conversation."

Upstairs, Scobie bent above Sammy and whispered, "Shh, it's all right." He picked him up and hugged him, stroking the fine hair on his soft head. "It's just fireworks, that's all. Look." He pointed through the window. The sky was burning, lighting their faces, Sammy's round eyes staring in stunned wonder at the spectacle. And then he fell asleep again, his eyelids fluttering, closing, opening quickly, gently closing. His head rested against Scobie's shoulder, his hands clenched Scobie's shirt. Carefully, Scobie lowered him back into his bed, covered his legs with the sheet, tucked his frayed toy giraffe under his arm, and tiptoed from the room. Susan rolled over onto her stomach and lay with her head resting in the cradle of her arm, waiting for him to appear through the screen door. Blades of grass, so close, looked like giant trees. How she missed the sea! Here he was. "Hello," he said, settling beside her. "Sammy's okay."

"You're a good father," she said.

"I'm learning."

"No, you've always been good."

"Hey, Joey," he said, changing the subject. "Did I ever tell you I once met John Lennon?"

"Bullshit, you met John Lennon."

"I did, really. In London. Nineteen sixty-six. I was on my way to see my parents. You know, for vacation, Christmas vacation. And there he was."

"Where?"

"At the airport bar. Disguised."

"Is he making all this up?" Joey asked Susan.

"I don't know."

"Disguised as what?" Clara asked.

"A tweedy literary type. His hair was slicked back, he was wearing a sort of gray sleeveless sweater. Thick glasses. Elbow patches. Those brown shoes that look like hiking boots, you know? We talked."

"I don't believe a word of this," Joey said.

"We talked about how we were both scared of flying. He was very nervous. Drinking."

For all Susan knew he was telling the truth. Stranger things had happened to him. On the other hand, he invented half his life. Which part of him did she love? He touched her knee affectionately. Why won't she respond? Why is she so cold? It angered him, briefly. He looked into the shaking light and saw Clara's hair, her round soft shoulders. The Roman candle sizzled and died. Susan felt like an old woman, some friendly but irritating third person. The sky was dark again, still and moist and starless.

"That was quick," she said.

"Actually, we've been out here six hours," Scobie said. "It's tomorrow."

"Seriously, wasn't that quick?" she asked.

"Yes," Clara said. "It was. I think."

"No, I'm on Scobie's side," Joey said. "Years have passed."

"Joey, stop it, you're making me nervous."

High up, far, far away, a small light moved through the sky.

. . .

Scobie made himself another Scotch.

"You're drinking too much," Susan said.

He raised his glass. "Quiet."

"What?"

"I thought I heard Sammy."

They both listened.

"No, he's all right," she said.

Scobie's arm had fallen asleep, a numb and prickly pain, but he did not move. "When you met me, what did you think?"

"That you were funny-looking."

"Thanks."

"It was your haircut."

"I cut it myself."

"That was apparent." She looked at him, shy and almost angry. "I *chased* you, Scobie. You should feel flattered."

The aquarium glowed, a green light through which the iridescent fish slowly circled the wavering seaweed and rising bubbles.

"Did you have a good time tonight?" she asked.

"Okay."

"I wish it would rain."

"Me, too." He traced her arm with a finger. "How come you're so skinny?"

"I have a pot belly," she said.

"The size of a walnut. You're skinny, Susan."

"You don't like me skinny?"

"I love you skinny."

"Is this true?"

"Yes," he said.

Her fingers stroked his skull as the room ticked around them, old complaints or the laughing dead. There's always someplace we're trying to get to, he thought. Something we're trying to remember or imagine. "Once, when we were little and wanted to have an adventure, Dad invented a spy game," he said. "The whole family played. Mom and I just missed catching him pass a secret message to Matthew at the drug store soda fountain."

"You romanticize your past."

"No, I don't. It happened. I know. I was there."

"You like it better."

"Oh, Susan. Don't exaggerate. I don't *like* it better."

"Yes, you do."

He pulled her closer. "What's the matter, baby?"

"Nothing."

"Susan?"

"You're itching to get away."

"Not me. I do all my traveling up here." He tapped his forehead, an absurd gesture.

"I'm sorry." Cold as a sudden draft, her hand touched his face. "I'm just jealous of Clara, I guess."

"What?" He felt himself blinking stupidly.

"I saw you tonight."

"What did you see tonight?"

"The way you looked at her."

"How did I look at her?"

"If you have feelings, you have feelings."

"Sweetheart, I love *you*." He realized he was slightly drunk.

"You can't avoid your guilt by not actually sleeping with Clara, then drive me crazy by making sure I know you'd like to. That's not fair, Scobie. I'm not stopping you."

He put *Nashville Skyline* on the turntable and sat back down beside her.

She sighed. "You really are going to leave me some day, aren't you?"

"I don't believe this. What's the matter with you?"

"I'm scared. Oh, Scobie, is this what you wanted?"

"Yes."

"Are you sure?"

"Yes," he said, though he was afraid of failure, afraid he might stop loving her.

"Let's go to bed," she said. "Okay?"

"I'm not sleepy."

"Well, I am." She stood, stretching her arms above her head. "Don't stay up too late."

"I won't."

She bent down and kissed him, her mouth soft and wide. "Good night."

"I love you."

"And I love you, Scobie."

She turned to climb the stairs, leaving behind an aura of desertion. Lighting a cigarette, he saw his own face in the window, the flare of the small flame briefly burning away his eyes. The walls were too white. He could not fill the space. He almost closed his eyes, but darkness seemed more frightening, an endless fall. The room taunted him, a parody of the rooms he had watched his parents soften and familiarize with their furniture, their habits, their laughter, their paintings. He missed them tonight. He wanted to ask them how they did it, how they made it through, for his own marriage now seemed as terrifying as this blank room. Why did he always feel he was doing something he had already done in another, more accurate life? He held on to his knees, trying to believe this version of reality. He could hear Susan upstairs as she moved toward the bathroom.

Water ran through the pipes. The sound reminded him of his grandparents' house, the small corner bedroom, his father's old room—the flowered wallpaper, the musty scent of rain, the desk by the window. He remembered winter nights returning from that house after Christmas, he and his brothers wrapped in blankets in the back seat, his mother and father talking quietly in front, the red glow of their cigarettes and the dim light of the dashboard, the sense of their world, small and self-contained, moving through the unfamiliar darkness, each gas station and motel a separate star, alien but no longer threatening, placed by distance as they sped home. He rose and walked into the kitchen. A copy of Kafka's stories lay on the table. He picked it up and stared at the photograph, Kafka's soft animal eyes, his complicated animal sadness. Upstairs, in the bedroom, Susan turned on the television, then flapped the sheets, smoothing all the wrinkles, before climbing into bed. Someone was talking about Jimmy Carter. Would he really be the next President?

"Scobie, come see!" Susan called.

"What?" He ran up the stairs.

"The news, the news. It's incredible."

"What's incredible?" he asked, hurrying into the bedroom.

She had pulled the sheets up to her chin. "Too late. You missed it."

"Missed what?" He looked at the television.

"Nothing." She blushed. "It was a trick. To get you up here."

"Why?"

"So we can make love."

"Oh, Susan." He laughed. "You're so strange."

Later, he thought he heard his father calling his name. He sat up in bed and stared into the darkness. There was nothing there.

"What's wrong?"
"I thought I heard something," he said.
"You've been hearing things all night."
He lay back down next to her. "Susan, let's have another kid. Sammy needs a sister. Okay?"
"Fine." She hugged him.
But he was already breathing deeply, his cheek resting on her shoulder. She stared at the trees outside caught by the corner streetlight, branches waving gently across the edges of her world. The weight of Scobie's body held her down, kept her from flying away. She could still remember the dark rooms in which she lay awake all night because the nuns had told her heaven was a hospital, eternity a white room with no windows, one soul to each room. Her parents, superstitious as peasants, had taught her the power of prayer. Order was the will to believe. Chaos was faithlessness. Out there beyond this room, this house, this family, a completely different way of thinking ruled the universe. Scobie was dreaming, twitching like a dog. She woke him. He grunted, rolled over, and soon she heard his quiet snore again. What had his parents taught him? Elegance, she thought. Elegance and desire. He had once told her he felt a moral obligation to disappoint them: "Every freedom has its costs." She rolled over, curling to the shape of his body, her breasts to his smooth back. She remembered a spot of light dancing across her eyes and her father's hands under her arms, teaching her to walk. Impossible. I can't

remember that far back. She tightened her arms around Scobie. He moved vaguely, slept. Sometimes they woke in the middle of the night making love. Midnight plunder, he called it. She wished they had enough money to visit her parents this summer. Why can't I sleep? What's wrong with me? Scobie's religion amounted to a fairy tale, a wistful disbelieving love for the power of wonder. She slipped her arm out from under him. Marriage was a compromise with terror. She arched her back, smoothing more wrinkles, the princess and the pea. Scobie snorted. She stroked his forehead. He wanted answers, not compromises. He *believed* in answers. But no mortal can give them, she thought. People invent ways to pass the time between birth and death, then invest them with absolute meaning. Yet all over America, right now, as heads sank softly into pillows, the same question rose in every imagination. Why? And the same black silence answered, no answer at all, just silence, the single separate person trapped inside the walls of her skull, no way out, no way to hear another voice and not suspect it's your own. The mind cannot investigate itself. What bright beauty could counter that? None. Facts were facts: the wrinkles around Scobie's eyes, the sadness at the corners of his mouth, his sudden, always unexpected ebullience as his long fingers and flat, wide palms lifted Sammy—squealing, delighted—into the air. Sweet, serious Sammy. His father's son. Her own love made visible. What would become of him? She slowly, carefully slipped from the bed. In a narrow shaft of light from the street she saw Scobie's sleeping face. A faint frown puzzled his forehead. Even in sleep he could not relax. She pulled the sheet to his chin. He curled, hands folded between his thighs. Tiptoeing, she left the room, still naked. Sammy's door was open, his room almost bleached by the light from the street. He lay on his stomach, a small pool of wetness by his mouth, his hands clenched into fists, subdued fury, his sheet kicked back and tangled at his feet. She covered him, brushed his damp hair from his forehead. Now what? She stood for a moment in the middle of the room, pondering a mysterious winking light—the glass eye of Sammy's toy giraffe. Quietly she returned to her own bed. All was well. Strange, she thought, how late at night your room becomes every room of your life. She lay flat on her back, her hands at her side, and closed her eyes. There was Scobie, only nineteen, smiling awkwardly from the dark dance floor, afraid, she later learned, to reveal his crooked teeth. He asked her to dance. His hands, she remembered, were damp, nervous, practically trembling as he held her at a respectful distance and spun her in a long slow waltz, or his version of one, a simple repetitive circle. Afterward, sweat cooling on her face, she walked with him through the sharp autumn night and he told her of his wandering childhood, his dream of becoming a writer, the cities he had seen. Time, too—he talked of time. On and on he went, talking, talking. She had never met anyone like him. So self-absorbed, so self-confident. All lies, she now knew. But then she could only see him bravely, her heart warming fast to this gloomy gentle stranger. From that night on she was addicted. She called it love, though she suspected that was only half the truth. The rest was recognition, finding someone so much like you he seems a brother, a shadow, an old, old friend. I could sleep with Joey, she thought. Then Scobie would know how it feels to see your lover made happy by someone else. As if you weren't there, as if you didn't exist. She also remembered the day

Sammy was born. She had just come in from the garden, a basket of squash and zucchini on her arm, when the pangs began, slowly at first, then gathering speed, urgency. She called Scobie. The moment had come. He gently led her to the car, helped her in, and moved around to the driver's seat, slowly and deliberately. Nor did he speed, he kept to the limit, cautiously maneuvering between other cars. Once, he turned and asked, "How are you?" Otherwise he was silent. This was happening much too fast, it wasn't right, would she lose the child? She closed her eyes and counted, recited the alphabet, spelled ten-syllable words, imagined the time when this would be a memory, reminded herself that a million million women had already passed through this moment and come out laughing, she raised and identified each finger. *Scobie, it hurts.* Had she said that, or merely thought it? When she opened her eyes Scobie was pulling into the hospital parking lot. Calmly he turned off the motor and guided her toward the swinging glass doors. Suddenly she felt fine. No pains. I panicked, she thought. It's not time yet. Silly fool. Then, direct as a rebuke, a line of searing heat severed her body. She nearly fainted. Scobie shouted something. He was holding her now, his arm around her shoulders. She heard running footsteps, a metallic rattling, the suck of soft shoes on tile. Hands rested her onto a cold hard surface. She was wheeled away, down hollow white hallways, into a room where Dr. Crawford appeared, efficiently giving orders. He bent and asked, "Ready?" Someone was trying to pull out all her teeth. *Where's Scobie?* "Here," his voice said. Then she felt his hands closing her eyes. "I'm right here, Susan. Everything's okay." He spoke from the bottom of an empty well. Someone else was drying her forehead with something cool.

Scobie's hand kept her eyes closed, thumb caressing her cheekbone. The pains were so close together now they merged into one pulsing roar. There was nothing left to count. "Push!" Dr. Crawford called. "Push, Susan." His hand massaged her belly. She heaved, slamming down, Scobie whispering into her ear, "I'm right here, I'm right here." Surely her stomach had started to tear, ripped like a fat pillow? And was that blood on her legs, dribbling, warm? The pain, a solid mass, began to move. She felt it, alive, her child swimming for the entrance through which half his consciousness had entered eight months earlier. She heard Scobie hiss, "Jesus Christ." Invisible hands pulled her legs apart, farther than they could spread. "Push!" Dr. Crawford sang. *"Push!"* She did, with all her might, every muscle she had, arching her back again. What happened next she really could not remember, except for the easing relief and the horrible fear her child might be dead. Then she started falling. She opened her eyes. The darkness had the quality of cloth. Where was she? Which room? When? "Scobie?" she whispered. But she and Sammy were back in New Hampshire. This was her sister's old room. Scobie had left her to live with Clara.

A Note on the Type

The text of this book was set on the Linotype in Garamond No. 3, a modern rendering of the type first cut by Claude Garamond (1510–1561). Garamond was a pupil of Geoffroy Tory and is believed to have based his letters on the Venetian models, although he introduced a number of important differences, and it is to him we owe the letter which we know as old-style. He gave to his letters a certain elegance and a feeling of movement that won for their creator an immediate reputation and the patronage of Francis I of France.

Composed by Fuller Typesetting of Lancaster, Lancaster, Pennsylvania
Printed and bound by The Haddon Craftsmen, Inc., Scranton, Pennsylvania